The

Intimates

THE
INTIMATES

Guy Mankowski

Legend 📖 Press
Independent Book Publisher

Legend Press Ltd, 2 London Wall Buildings,
London EC2M 5UU
info@legend-paperbooks.co.uk
www.legendpress.co.uk

British Library Cataloguing in Publication Data available.

ISBN 978-1-9077564-6-7

Edited by: Lauren Parsons-Wolff

Set in Times
Printed by JF Print Ltd., Sparkford.

Cover designed by Gudrun Jobst
www.yotedesign.com

Legend ◗ Press

Independent Book Publisher

Acknowledgements

I'd firstly like to thank Rhian and Tom Lewis, as without their generosity I would never have had the means to write this book.

Lauren Parsons-Wolff first suggested that I develop this story from a novella into its current form, and I'm hugely grateful for the passion, enthusiasm and understanding that she showed while overseeing the editing process. Tom Chalmers and Lucy Boguslawski also played a big role in developing me from a short story writer and I'm grateful to them.

My family – Vivienne, Andrew and Oliver Mankowski, and Stanley and Shirley Firmin have been extremely support-ive of my writing from when I was scrawling stories as a young boy.

As readers Quey Craddock, Jamie Burn, Jeremy Bradfield and Hal Branson were also supportive, often at critical junctures. I'm very appreciative of the technical advice Peter Walker offered; to have the support of such an established writer at an early stage was a great boost. I'm grateful also to Joan Deitch at Pollinger for pushing me to take my writing more seriously. Gary Murning has been something of an unofficial mentor to me throughout the process; his Machiavellian attitude towards self-promotion has given me an assertiveness I otherwise would not have possessed.

I would lastly like to thank Elise, who is so different to her namesake, and who without a doubt inspired *The Intimates*.

To Vivienne and Andrew Mankowski, with love.

The pool had long been drained of any water. All that filled it now were leaves, brittle and gold in the bright morning sun. When I opened my eyes I saw the hollow shell of the pool, its walls stained with algae. I realised that I wasn't alone in its corner, as huddled against my torn tuxedo was a pale girl with dark hair, asleep.

I had no idea where I was, or how I had arrived there. The only feeling I had was one of slight post-coital nausea, the instinctive guilt a lapsed Catholic feels when waking up next to a stranger. My opening eyes passed over statues covered with vines, which had seemingly never been disturbed. I recognised nothing in the garden. When the girl in my arms stirred as if to awake, something told me she would offer more questions than answers. What follows are the thoughts that scrolled across my mind as I recalled the evening that had just passed.

The morning sun makes me remember lights. The feeling of it against my eyes reminds me of torches illuminating the lawn. Evening gowns flitted past, through shadows cast by statues. Laughter rose and faded like applause, passing through the evening, accompanied by the sound of clinking glasses. I remember champagne spilt on ivory carpets, pianos rippling through the summer's night.

Slowly faces emerged, at first only as delicate sensations, slightly preserved memories. Some appeared clearer than others. They were seated around a mahogany table, each glistening under a chandelier. Sequins sparkled as profiles creased with laughter. I saw sheaths of paper, a finished manuscript, a book perhaps? I had the feeling that I was in the company of special people, that I was recalling an important night. That it had been a somehow wonderful, yet eventually terrible night. What had brought us all together? Eight faces were seated around the table clad in evening dress, picking at delicacies, sipping wine and laughing. The emotions they provoked in me swam back first, followed by their names, and then each of their tragic stories. And as these details slowly emerged, I realised that in some way I was attached to every single one of them.

The first was Francoise, an elegant woman in her late forties. Something about her arrested my attention before all others. It wasn't just that she was the hostess. I gained the sense that she herself had grown assured of her unique appeal with time. Perhaps she had recently achieved something? I recall her as a slim figure in a black dress, her kind face full of Gallic beauty as she strokes the heads of her three dogs, each competing for her attention as she sits down. She had a soft French accent that enhanced the aura created by the warm lights. She smiled kindly at a butler before lowering her pastel lips to a flame offered by him. She held the cigarette in her slender fingers, inhaled deeply, and then blew perfumed smoke up in a fine jet at the glass icicles above her. I remember watching it cloud there, before curling amongst itself and fading. Her eyes met mine, and she smiled at me with a mixture of coyness and bravado, before looking slowly around at her guests. My eyes fixed on hers, also fascinated by each guest in turn, and I noticed how she refrained from speaking until their words had somehow satisfied her. There was a quiet power in her restraint, as if she knew exactly how her withdrawal would benefit the evening.

To her left sat an angular man with a familiar face, one that may have seemed cruel to others and yet the remembrance of Graham is comforting to me. I recall how exactly he held his wine glass, as if it was an instrument to be employed with precision. As I picture his hand I see flashes of red nail varnish on the tips of his fingers, and as his face moves into the light a smear of glitter illuminates his cheeks. He is poised, aloof, and yet his arch demeanour in my eyes is nothing more than mischievous. As I recall his long fingers he looks up at me with a smile, and something sparkles around his lips. But only for a moment, before his attention is transferred to the cloud of conversation being steamed by other guests.

At his side sat Georgina, a vivacious woman who expressed herself using her hands and her generous smile. Her hair was tousled into a stylish swirl, her lips pouted when she laughed. She was at once childlike and voluptuous, wearing a sky blue dress, an arc of diamonds illuminating her neck. Unlike the man to her left, she had a calm likeability, a look of someone brought up in the warmth of foreign holidays, taught perhaps by the most reassuringly expensive voices.

The man next to her looked as though money had been bestowed on him when he lacked the maturity to let it take care of him. Franz's skin was a bright copper colour, as if it had been blasted with sun to promote the illusion of health. He wore an expensive silk shirt, and yet remained the type of man who looked roguish even in evening wear. A cigar bristled in his fingers, but as he sprinkled ash around him it was apparent that he was not altogether comfortable with it. I noticed that the tips of his fingers were chafed, as if they had spent years persuading steel guitar strings to stay down. When I look at him he doesn't return my gaze, as I'm sure he once would have. He seems occupied with involving himself in any conversation, even when he has nothing to contribute. He spent a great deal of time looking at the blonde woman next to him who is now returning my gaze.

Elise had small, cold features and bright red lips, and her profile was almost aquiline. She carried herself resolutely, as if she'd decided to be beautiful, and in doing so had almost become so. Her slim body was wrapped in a red dress, and a shawl hung around her small shoulders, which were beginning to lose their winter paleness. Her hair was pretty but thin, a sharp lock of it cutting across her forehead. In my memory she is almost doll-like, occasionally resembling a girl dressed as a woman, but the thought of her is still somehow erotic to me. But this feeling is tempered with a sense of clamminess, the belief that our bond has not developed naturally, but more out of determination on her part. When Franz becomes animated she twitches her fingers, reaching to hold my hand under the table. But the act does not seem spontaneous or smooth. The way she grasps my hand evokes a sense of claustrophobia, a feeling which I realise is becoming increasingly familiar around her. The conspiratorial look she gives me, at once frightened and exhilarated, suggests not just that we have come together but also that she is separate from the others. I recall the feeling that she often demands protection from me in social situations, protection which is unnecessary but ensures that she can cling to me throughout.

Next to her is a much older woman, although I sense that she would object to this description. To the passing eye she appears a ravishing buxom blonde, but on further inspection she lacks Francoise's grace. Her hair is bright platinum gold and her slightly aged fingers appear expensively manicured. Her dress seems designed especially to push her slightly withering cleavage forward. Despite her loud and frequent laughs, she is able to only adjust herself in small movements, suggesting she is wedged in by a tight corset. I sense from her constant bustling and pouting that she feels a need to assert herself, and then I remember she is the only one of us from an older generation. Her name is Barbara, and after she tells Elise this she looks away guiltily. Before moving my gaze to her neighbour I see that her face has a plastic stillness to it. She is now laughing coquettishly with the peculiar man at her right, whose nails appear driven to the bone.

He had the weary, tense look of someone wired to a grid, perhaps aware he's at the constant mercy of the next burst of electricity he might receive. His veined arms suggest an artistic temperament, which has perhaps become more of a duty than a pleasure. The hairs on his hands are flecked with paint, and his slightly open shirt reveals a sun-starved chest. His name is James and, although he smiled weakly at the other guests around him, he retained the pained look of a martyr, of someone who spends a great deal of time alone. When he finally turns to face me, I recall the shock on seeing that his eyes appear covered in thick white paste; I remember that he is blind. Perhaps this explains why he does not feel embarrassed at his constant consideration of the woman at his right, unlike me.

An egotistic feeling tells me I'll find that it is her in my arms. Her name's Carina, she has Mediterranean looks and intense, knowing eyes. In the way she remains above conversations, never indulging the men who try to engage her, it seems she's aware of the power she gains through restraint. My memories of how she looked in the early evening are vague, as I only ever stole glances at her, reluctant to reveal how she'd intrigued me. She wore a black dress with a diamond broach that glittered in the candlelight. Somehow its multi-faceted glare seemed garish next to the subtle swirl of colours on the skin below her neck. Her flawless hair was lit into a bright sheen by the chandelier above her. She had the manner of someone bored of being told she's beautiful. I recognise the feeling she provokes in me immediately. She is one of those enchanting people we sometimes meet who perhaps intentionally divulge little so that we remember much about them. Flitting figures like her enthral and frustrate; they reveal enough to suggest an essence you could chase for a lifetime, but reveal so little that they render that quest ridiculous. When I spoke to her at the table she replied in short, staccato sentences, long enough to allow engagement but short enough to prevent her revealing anything. Yet when I busied myself with a wineglass, or turned my attention to someone else, I felt the glare of her eyes on the side of my face. Something about the way her eyes looked through me suggested she had considered me for a long time. Yet despite these peculiarly intimate glances she seemed keen to keep that a secret. As a result we exchanged looks that seemed intended to make the other feel as if we had dismissed them. I wondered if an opportunity had once arose to open ourselves up to each other, a window that had blazed open for only a few moments before being shut snapped by a fear of admitting something that might cast us in a mutually vulnerable light. The tension between us suggested that for many years we had stayed on this trapeze with one another, familiar enough to imply closeness but distant enough to suggest this was merely circumstantial.

Carina spoke very little at the table, and the few words that she did utter there now possess a certain resonance. I only remember her saying one line while we were seated. I can't remember its context or why it stands out, but I can recall the slight air of melancholy when she said: "I've lost whatever it takes to stay a girl, without gaining whatever is needed to be a woman".

One other feeling occurs to me in tandem with the memory of those characters. It's a feeling of intimacy, and that word itself seems to possess grave importance. This was not merely a dinner party; this was a celebration of intimacy, with Francoise as its centrepiece. I turned her image round in my mind; I examined it from various angles. I remember the way she held a cigar for Franz as though it was an expensive pen, and then I remember that she is a writer, and what's more this party was held to celebrate the recent publication of her first novel. Francoise had lived a decadent lifestyle of luxury, had frittered her life away on weightless pleasures, and this book, *The Intimates*, was her sole achievement. It had been started eight years ago about this group of people she met when returning belatedly to university, and had been finally published in the early summer that beckoned in that evening. It described seven men and women whose futures had glistened with potential. Francoise, Carina, James, Franz, Graham, Georgina and me; seven people who had since failed to deal with the weight of expectation laid upon their shoulders. Who had each failed to do justice to the cursed gifts that had briefly offered each of us a passage to transcendence.

Although the night was a celebration of her success, it did seem tinged with a potent sadness. Perhaps someone had been unable to make it? Passing over those faces, so familiar and yet still so foreign, it occurred to me that the sadness was amongst us, The Intimates. Looking at the seven faces I saw that they all carried a certain melancholy; a sense of remorse hung over the proceedings like a ghost. Our times had passed, our glistening careers hadn't blossomed, and we had not become the people we'd once seemed destined to be. We shared a key characteristic with certain people born into the world on a seemingly arbitrary basis – we were marked. We had been expected to bend our lives towards the creation of everything unique. And yet looking at the forced happiness on each face, it was apparent that every one of us had conspicuously failed to achieve this, and now it dogged us permanently. Our shared destinies were a weight coiled round our necks, which only grew heavier with time. A maid leant over Francoise, holding a tray of drinks. She smiled sympathetically, and for a second I wondered if she knew our curse. This expectation, inherited to us and encouraged by the world, was a gift if we matched its demands, but a curse if we left it to flounder. Tonight, even in the light of Francoise's recent success, it seemed brutal to create an evening with which to confront us with our failures. If that had not in fact been Francoise's intention, then it was still how it felt.

At the table it seemed that this weight was not the only factor weighing upon the minds of The Intimates. As Francoise smiles up at her butler, assuring him the evening is unfurling to plan, I remember why this is the case. This evening she's to finally read us the opening chapter of her book, and in effect open a time capsule to each of our pasts. Even in the early evening I can feel a sense of trepidation amongst us seven. Although Francoise at this moment has a gentility that seems without threat, the looks exchanged between us suggest that we are all aware of how stinging her portraits of us might be. The glances we each exchange are ones of gathering fear.

I remember looking round those faces, each busy with their own façades, and feeling a little nauseous. Elise saw the look of shame on my face and placed her hand on my thigh. But that only made it worse. She didn't share this guilt; she wasn't condemned. Her comfort seemed to be a mocking message from another world, where this weight only existed in light sympathy. I'd achieved nothing, I remember thinking. And an evening had been organised especially to drive that knife home.

My thoughts were disturbed by the sound of clinking glass, which cut across the babble of conversation, smothering it. Francoise was rising to her feet, a faint smile on her face. People elbowed one another into silence, every face craned up at her. Basking in the light of this attention she assumed an elegant pose.

"Friends," she began, smiling warmly around her. "*Thank you* for coming tonight to share this wonderful evening with me. And Elise; I'm glad that you could join us too. As you know, *The Intimates* was inspired by the six of you, who I met when I finally began a university education – the last wish of my father just before he passed away. Some of you had been close since childhood, but I came to join this unusual group later in life. In time each of you became as precious to me as a family member, without the attending conceit that so often affects such bonds." The guests tittered politely.

"I had left school at eighteen," she continued, "and as a daughter of privilege I had been given the room to indulge myself at a time when many are consumed with establishing a stable footing in the world. My sole achievement was a controversial journal article I'd written, satirising the harmless pretensions of my father's friends. Amongst that affluent little group it caused quite a stir – with its pointed caricatures and waspish observations. It offered me brief celebrity status and the opportunity to enjoy a few years masquerading as a novelist, while lazing about on boats. Fortunately, on my return to university this appetite for decadence was quenched when I met the seven of you. Inspired, for the first time in years I started to write a book which many years later would become *The Intimates*. I wrote it as a shrine to an intriguing time of my life and to an enchanting set of artists. See it simply as a testament to each of your wonderful talents. It occurs to me this evening how naïvely it was written; I hope that you bear this in mind when I present my dusty portraits of each of you later on tonight. But perhaps its naïvety lends it some charm.

"At that time Franz was starting to light up the world with his gift for music, having encouraged each of us to address our talents. While Barbara was taking on the world of film, her daughter was becoming drawn to the stage. This interest had begun in her childhood when Vincent wrote plays for the two of them to act out in his garden." Georgina smiled at me, and I felt myself blush with the attention. The guests laughed, and Elise squeezed my hand. "Vincent too had begun to find ways to express his potential, and James and Graham had started to bow to the evidence that they had something unique to offer.

Since then life has taken each of us on a course, which I could not have predicted, which I was naïve to prematurely prescribe. As a young woman I felt my writing contained a watermark of destiny, but I now see that as the arrogance of youth. My predictions for each of you were deeply flawed, and the blame for that inaccuracy lies purely with me. As I spend time in your company I realise that my portrayals could never have done any of you justice. Each of you has blossomed in myriad ways I could not have foreseen, with a versatility the world can encompass but that my adolescent worldview could not. So tonight let us celebrate that, and let us celebrate too a rare evening together, to warm ourselves against the chill of passing time. I am privileged that each of you have returned for an evening in my company, to celebrate perhaps the only piece of work I will ever be determined to finish." At this the guests laughed generously.

Francoise raised her glass. "To The Intimates," she toasted. "*The Intimates*," came the echo; Elise's voice a step behind the rest.

I took a sip of wine, felt its curious effect begin to take hold. What was restraining my thoughts from returning fully, permitting them to only stumble into my consciousness? Was it sleep, or wine that spread itself like a film over my mind's eye?

I remember the music that struck up as the guests sipped wine after dinner. When it started to fill the room I saw Barbara start, her tight face stifling an indignant anger. Francoise had urged her maid to play one of the vinyl's kept by the gramophone, and without meaning to offend the maid had put on the soundtrack to *Double Cross*, not knowing it was the box office flop which had ended Barbara's acting career. The compressed anger in Barbara's face was obscured by the lull of that music, which carried my mind's eye to another scene.

It was a similar song, a gypsy waltz stuffed with accordions which I'd heard as I stepped through a cobbled street. Musicians were pressed against a wall, swaying as they pumped their instruments in the early summer evening. Adrenalin had seeped through me, spurred on by the abandon of the music. I'd passed a bed of roses that bristled in the warm wind. A hopeful feeling told me I was meeting a girl, but an aftertaste told me that my father might be joining us too.

I was dressed in a new suit, carrying lilies, walking through the outskirts of a city. The open shutters above me flapped out from ochre buildings, reminding me of Florence. The music faded quickly as I cut down an empty street, seeing a café bordered with ivy. Women were laughing with brooding boyfriends as they stepped into the square, arm in arm. I smiled at a waitress as I passed into the diner. I sat for a while on the balcony there, watching the people pass, thinking how my life seemed to charge itself with visits to such effervescent places. I sipped a glass of red wine as I waited, watching housewives stop their bicycles to chatter to one another as dusk descended.

I recall looking for a flash of red in the distance, listening for the clack of high heels. Soon Elise steps cautiously onto the balcony, this time in a delicate summer dress that exposes her slim arms. At this moment it occurs to me how differently Elise is portrayed in this memory than at the party. It's as if an invisible film separates the two images. A film that I can't break through. On the roof garden she seems caught up in the pleasures of the world. Perhaps she is relieved, relieved that she's met a man so keen for her to open up. As I recall her walking over to me I remember the overarching emotion being one of hope. That tonight I would prompt her to uncoil, but the time would soon come when she would do the same to me. I wonder if since that night, rather than reciprocating, she has instead learnt to cling. Watching this memory I therefore cannot help but feel a sense of nostalgia.

She smiles warmly when she sees me, and I see her face is carefully made-up. She's wearing her favourite French perfume, the scent of which always culminates in desire. She kisses my cheek as the waiter gestures for her to sit opposite me, with a very Italian flourish. The moment the waiter turns away I pull her into me and her face breaks into a smile. She warns me not to smear her lipstick, but then thinking better of it she kisses me lightly on the cheek.

From our seats we can see the city bustle in its colours below. With quick, slim fingers she tears off strips of bread and sprinkles them with olive oil. I'm glad to be in her company, she makes me feel relaxed and open. She laughs generously, her hand touches my waist, and she looks up at me through long, dark lashes. If I overstep the mark she retreats into her chair, and I long to capture with a camera the moments when she considers the city below, unmasked in her seat. I urge myself to make her laugh more, and as I do I ease gradually towards her, my mouth approaching the nape of her neck. She laughs knowingly, and the very English elegance in her smile is a sight I want to preserve as I know I will experience it all too briefly. I snatch a kiss at her neck and she pushes me gently away, but I've preserved that smile a little longer. I provoke her, tease her, admonish her to unwind and she does gradually, as bottles of wine come and go. I earn intimacy with her, ducking and diving and pushing with words, and when her revealing eventually occurs I step back and bask in it. I feel I am where I should be, opposite a petite woman with red lips, high above a colourful city.

Just before my father arrives I realise I have worked to make her laugh in the hope that it will be her primary memory of the evening. I find myself looking repeatedly at my watch. "He'll be here any minute now," I say, and she takes three sharp sips of wine, suddenly looking very vulnerable. She has never met him before.

My father has an unerring ability to make even the most comfortable places feel hostile. He bristles with indignation if the wine isn't precisely the right temperature. He retracts into moody silences if a topic isn't expanded in enough detail, and smiles in a long-suffering manner if you try to steer the conversation in a direction he is reluctant to go. Merely sitting opposite him is an exhausting experience. His many pregnant pauses, his readiness to disrupt the flow of someone else's thought, and the way he refuses to acknowledge certain remarks is all very draining. The words of the many people who have told me he's the great playwright of our time often linger in my ears, but they're never enough to dispel the discomfort I feel in his presence. I often remind myself of how fortunate I am to be his son, but in an instant that feeling turns to resentment the moment he arrives.

Elise snaps open a compact to check her lips, as I sense him move onto the balcony. The waiter is bent deferentially over, but my father ignores him, one hand in his blazer pocket as he makes his way over to us. Elise steps to her feet, rather too quickly, and he moves back as if surprised by her assertiveness. I tell myself to remain seated. There is a look on his face that's at once bemused and distant.

"This is Elise."

"Elise Zielifski, isn't it?" he says, without a smile.

"Yes, it is," she answers.

"Are you descended from Polish Jews?" he asks, and she gathers herself as he sits down.

"I am."

He pauses, for so long that I wonder if she could have made such an innocuous remark differently. "Did you hear what she said?" I ask.

"My son, Vincent, is a lapsed Catholic," he says, waving a hand at me. "Your mother would be intrigued by this match. Wouldn't she Vincent?" The waiter appears behind him. "I'll have an '87 Rioja."

"How is the new play coming on?" I ask him.

"People ask me that question as though my trials are something I like to reflect upon in my spare time, and they're not," he snaps. "The stage decorators are incompetent, the producer is a dilettante, and the actors would be far more comfortable in a circus. It's an endurance test, like so many things, and as the writer I endure more than anyone. If Anthony was not directing it the whole affair would be quite beyond the pale. He's the only one there who shares my passion for hard work you see; though even he has insisted I take a short break from it all this evening. But he'll be here before long, to draw me back towards the theatre. Apparently he's the only one there with enough spine to take on that duty."

"Elise is a teacher," I offer. "In the city."

"Is that so? Who do you teach, children in the ghetto?"

"She's a primary school teacher."

"She can tell me that."

Her eyes pass between the two of us.

"It's a good school," she says. "The parents teach their children in their spare time so much that I sometimes feel I'm just offering them an education supplement."

I close my eyes, wishing I'd advised her to always answer his questions objectively.

"How long have you been friends?" he eventually asks, looking at me.

"We're dating." I answer.

"We met eight weeks ago, at a concert," Elise replies. "He had to ask me out four times before I agreed."

"And did you find that flattering?" he asks. Elise shrugs, with a confused look. "A lesser woman may have perceived him as a man with few options." He flashes a smile.

"Thanks," she says. "Vincent talks about you all the time. I'm trying to persuade him to show you some of his recent writing."

"And have you been successful so far?"

"It's an ongoing discussion," I say.

He sits back in his chair. "Vincent feels my criticisms of his work are needlessly in-depth and elaborate." He leans into Elise and with a hoarse stage-whisper, "I think he finds my advice boring."

"More relentless than boring." I regret my words as soon as they have left my mouth. Within moments, swilling wine around his glass, he is imparting brusque criticisms in a stately tone while looking around him for agreement.

"I've said before Vincent, in a piece of writing you *must* postpone it's pinnacle, you *must* make your reader earn that climax, and yet you fritter it away in the preamble, so that when you connect those threads at the peak you make only a minor hill, when a mountain was more than necessary." Elise retracts. "In a debate I imagine your arguments would begin with the strongest, and then progressively weaken. Your opponent would sense your strongest argument had dribbled out of you, and he'd crush you, like that." He thumps his hand on the table, making Elise jump, before reaching for his wine.

"Writing is the same; *you* have the absolute knowledge in the palm of your hand. You *must* refrain from revealing yourself – and seduce them with it. We've talked about this before, and yet you are never prepared to listen to me."

"Please keep your voice down. People are looking at us."

"But you don't," he continues. "Your writings lack the conviction of eventual resolution. They are like the ill-informed ramblings of the bourgeois." He spat each word bitterly into his glass. I kept my eyes fixed on him.

"Many struggling young writers would chew off their arm to have a father like me, to point out the flaws in their work. Yet you find me so utterly redundant. Really Elise, you should speak to him about this. He finds his old man such a tiresome bore."

Elise opens her mouth and draws breath, but I sense that she realises there is nothing helpful she could say at this point.

"Do you not agree with me either?" he snaps, when she closes her mouth without speaking.

"Please don't bring her into our disagreements."

"It's a healthy debate Vincent. A rigorous bit of verbal rough and tumble. She teaches disenchanted children in the back alleys of our cities, I'm sure she can handle a little jousting."

Elise smiles a little, but looks away. "Perhaps after a few more glasses," she says.

"So she needs drink to assert herself? What an interesting woman."

I grip the menu and glower at him over the top of it. He sees my eyes burning in his direction, but he refuses to meet them. His eyes flicker in saccadic movements over the contents of the menu.

"I can see you staring at me Vincent," he says, not meeting my eye. The waiter comes to collect our order. "Relax. No-one can hear us."

I decide I will not speak to him until he apologises for his treatment of Elise. He's found an insidious new way to undermine my judgement, and used her in order to do so. But just as I am rallying my thoughts on how to counteract this, I see Anthony's tall and rather stooped figure enter the balcony. My father raises his eyebrows in relief and he sets down the menu.

"You must remember Anthony, Vincent?" my father asks, as his friend stops in front of our table, fixing his penetrating gaze on Elise.

"He was very young when we last met," Anthony says.

"It was nine months ago," I answer, turning my attention down to the menu.

"Anthony, as usual, is quite correct in that case," my father replies. Elise looks quizzically between the two men, and then concernedly at me.

The two of them grasp hands and my father waves him towards a vacant chair. "I think we are just about able to accommodate you."

Anthony looks disdainfully down at the seat, and cocks his head as he considers Elise.

"This is Elise Zielifski," I say. "Elise, my father's main confidante, Anthony."

"Zielifski?" Anthony says, hovering over the seat for a second. "How interesting."

"I know. Anthony, do you have time to join us for a rather warm glass of Rioja?" my father asks.

Anthony leans forward as if steeling himself. "It is my unfortunate duty, Sean, to insist that we return to the theatre now for a post-matinee discussion. I fear that imbibing any wine will only render the meeting less constructive. I hope you have been able to catch up with your son as you intended?" Anthony lowers his gaze onto me and back onto my father. The way he slowly straightens up suggests that he has already drawn his own conclusions about this.

My father laughs. "You are a hard task master, Anthony. But sadly, no. I have only been with my son for a few minutes, and I suspect that I already could have handled our reunion better."

"I'm sure that any tensions can be explained by the generation gap," Anthony answers. "Which these two are more responsible than you for defining."

Now feeling a burning sense of injustice, I fix my eyes on the cityscape. Elise begins to ask the two of them cautious questions about their play.

The flower beds below suddenly seem to teem with energy, and they smear into a haze as I look down on them. The sensation of them pressing against my eyes brings me back to the fairy lights on the balcony at Francoise's party – which similarly blurred my vision as I gazed at them.

They illuminate our profiles as I look down at the little boats on the pond below. Each has a small, lighted candle inside them. They pass through each other, like a gold constellation dissolving amongst itself on top of a black lake. The rich scent of wine fills the air as Georgina moves past me, dancing to the faint music in the background. She stops and looks at me with an inquisitive smile. The lamps on the balcony light the edges of her hair. The lack of focus I have at this point suggests that I've started to feel the drink. We are over the essential point any good party advances towards, where each guest has gained enough confidence from their surroundings to fall into synch with their company. They've joined the rhythm of the group, which adjusts slightly for each new addition, granting each guest the opportunity to shed their individuality for a while. As this ephemeral mark is passed each guest is answerable only to the oscillations of the party. Recklessness and impulsivity have become de rigueur, and hardly a consequence of individual thought.

A butler is pouring a bottle of champagne onto a pyramid of crystal glasses, and I watch the golden liquid bubble and foam, dancing around the rims as it splashes down to a bed of ice. Franz offers a glass to Carina, trying subtly to make her laugh, but she only smiles politely, sipping her glass and looking into the distance. Francoise, her voice tinged with the nonchalance of someone used to lounging around St. Tropez in late spring, is telling James that she believes her garden is haunted. "At this time of night," she whispers, her eyes looking up at him brightly, "it is so easy to believe. When I bought the house the last owner told me strange things happen in this garden. Perhaps if we stay close, and watch carefully, something will start to unfold, no?" I know her mystical words are all part of a seductive act, but looking down at those lights, seemingly dancing to some inaudible music, it does seem almost feasible. There is something enchanting about the way she seems to genuinely believe her fantasies.

"Francoise, you should keep your imaginings for your writing." Georgina says.

"Vincent believes me, don't you?" Francoise insists, waving towards me. "Vincent pretends to be so cynical, but his mind is alive with possibilities, isn't it true? He inherits that from his father."

Georgina looks carefully at me as I smile, aware of many eyes on me. "It must be one of the few things we do share."

Georgina laughs dryly, blushing on my behalf. "He's being modest. You've embarrassed him!"

The hostess chuckles to herself and places a glass in my hand. "Your father is in the country at the moment, isn't he? Perhaps he will surprise us with a visit tonight."

"Don't tease him," Georgina says.

"You wouldn't do that to me," I say to Francoise. She holds my gaze and then looks bemused.

I can see on the grass below us seven ice sculptures, slender and glassy, contrasted against the inky black of the garden. A creamy cloud surrounds them, from the steam rising off their bodies. The drink suddenly possesses me, and for a second it appears that one of them is moving nearer to me, advancing clumsily in our direction before settling back into its icy frame.

"It is a strange evening, isn't it?" Georgina whispers, as her scent passes behind me. I steady myself as she moves to my side. "These early summer nights have a mercurial quality unlike any other time of year. It makes my mind shimmer with possibilities." I look up, surprised at how close to her I suddenly feel. She smiles, holding my gaze for a second, and then looks over the edge of the balcony.

"The feeling I get at the start of the summer never ceases to amaze me. It's as if the world shrugs off its shrouds, no longer bashful about how beautiful it is." I smile in a way which I hope shows agreement. "If it's any comfort, I think you are the opposite of your father," she then says; as if acknowledging something that's plaguing me.

"I find that quite comforting."

She meets my eye and smiles. "We are so similar, you and I. We are both expected to be pleased to live in a parent's shadow. As if it is some mighty achievement just to be spawned by someone the public recognises!" She sips her glass three times in quick succession, as though steeling herself from this thought.

"I agree. My father's legacy is a tricky thing to constantly run from. Unlike most men, who merely have to achieve something, I have to write three masterpieces instead of his mere two before I can have any impact on the world."

"Yes." Her eyes pass over to Barbara, who is laughing loudly at a card trick Franz is showing her. Barbara pretends to find his awkwardness amusing and clasps her hands to his arm. Franz looks back at her with a steeliness that is quite disconcerting. Barbara drapes her arm across his shoulder before Franz looks over at the two of us, suddenly caught by Georgina's gaze, as his fingers reach up to hold her mother's hand. Georgina looks away sharply. A breeze lifts the curls from her shoulder, exposing the pale skin on her neck. She suddenly looks very vulnerable. "Isn't she a little old to be a groupie? And isn't Franz a little too familiar with her to be this easily seduced?"

"Perhaps she just likes being the centre of attention."

"She's always *had* to be the centre of attention. At least your father actually achieved something. I mean, like you I'm not a fan of his work. Too self-important and heavy for me. But unlike my mother, he did at least achieve his potential. She's so obsessed with who she might have been."

I turn my head away from Barbara, and notice how little her daughter resembles her. "Well she made three films, didn't she? They did reasonably well, didn't they?"

"I suppose. But were they in any way memorable? I think it's better to leave an undiscovered batch of outsider art than a familiar bundle of mediocrity. Were her films, in any way, art?" A pause hangs in the air. We both catch each others eye and laugh quickly, as if the same thought has occurred to both of us but should not be said.

"I can't sit through them," she hisses, leaning back. "Those terrible, sexist light comedies. She was just a pale imitation of Anita Ekberg, making sure her cleavage was on show as she laughed coquettishly throughout. At least with Marilyn Monroe you got a sense of compromised intellect. With my mother…" she pauses as Barbara whoops at another failed card trick, "there's nothing behind the eyes. She represents to me the shabbiest type of film, where achieving the demands its surface requires, supersedes the importance of creating any resonance. At least your father created work of some substance. In total she achieved nothing, and yet I'm forced to live in the shadow of it. The shadow of nothing."

"He loves the thought that my achievements will never equal his," I respond without missing a beat. Her eyes widen, as if she recognises this nascent anger. "He lambastes whatever writing of mine he can get his hands on, with criticisms hollow enough to always be entirely unconstructive."

"They don't want us to do well, do they? My mother wouldn't even *let* me be an actress. It scared her that I was so literate; she couldn't get her head around it. She says she was just concerned that showbiz would chew me up and spit me out, but I know now she was just so scared that I might make a success of it. She talks about the world of cinema as if it's a conquest. A past lover, clamouring to get back in through the window. But the truth is, once she fell pregnant with my brother and I, the offers dried up. Straight away. Her appeal was as an untarnished, sexy girl-next-door. The idea of her having a family clashed too much with her image. Her window of opportunity passed... thanks to me and him."

I watch Barbara pulling her dress behind her, sticking her breasts out over the balcony as Franz chases her. She is laughing uproariously, as though thoroughly enjoying a man giving her his undivided attention. "Francoise wants us to play some party games later, which will doubtless involve a little acting. Did you see my mother's eyes light up when she suggested it? She'll play every part as if it's the title role in *Some Like It Hot*. We'll see more of her cleavage than is strictly necessary throughout it, and she'll embarrass me. I promise you, all of those things will happen."

I pause for a second, as both of us watch the grim flirtation between Franz and her mother play out.

"Do you ever feel like she gives you a hard time for just being born?" I whisper, half-hoping my words will be drowned out by Barbara's laughter.

"Yes. *Yes.* Even now. 'An actress' figure cannot *endure* childbirth,' she says. 'My time ended the moment I had you both.'" Georgina hisses the words, her voice a prissy caricature of her mother's. "She doesn't even mention my brother; we barely ever talk about him anymore."

"He died just after you were both born, didn't he?"

"Yes. But it's as if he never happened. She wasn't ready to be a mother, and didn't want to be, and he died weeks after coming into the world. His death was just the first barrier between me and her."

"I'm sorry," I say. "Relationships with parents are almost always difficult."

She nods her agreement. "What about your father? Does he ever support your writing?"

I quote his comments on my last piece precisely. It surprises me how exact the memory of insult is. The tone, the inflections, the emphases. Georgina laughs sympathetically, throwing her hair back – which in my memory splays over the light from the lamp behind her. It stays there like a snapshot, the fine gossamers layered against the canvas of the rich, dark sky. When the sensations from that moment have settled I look back at her, clutching a cocktail to her chest, her head bowed as she watches Franz circle her mother. "Don't stand here watching them," I admonish. "Do you remember the summer house down in Francoise's garden?" My words tear her from her preoccupation for a second and she smiles, as if arrested by the arrival of comforting memory.

"Do you think it is still there?" she asks, a little guiltily.

"Let's find out."

As I walk deeper into the garden, I remember how Georgina and I had been the first to arrive at The Fountains that afternoon. The two of us had stayed out on that lawn for as long as we could, until Francoise drew us inside, away from the fading heat.

It had felt good that afternoon to leave my usual routine. As I walked onto the sunlit lawn of The Fountains I felt as if I had entered a sanctuary. Though I usually felt taunted by uncertainty, here it no longer seemed pertinent. To reside in that house for one evening made me believe it inevitable that one day all my ambitions would be fulfilled; that my time outside The Fountains was a mere testing ground. It seemed I had returned home, to a place where all the usual questions were now irrelevant.

Seeing Francoise reclining on the lawn, sipping a glass of iced tea with the sun on her face, I felt I had entered a world of elegance which I could only be privy to by possessing some talent. I knew then that over the course of the party I would try to find a way to permanently inhabit this world. I suspected that by giving me a glimpse of what success might offer, Francoise had encouraged such rumination. As the gates closed behind me, sealing away my problems for one glorious evening, Georgina waved a tennis racket in my direction and Francoise peered up from the wide rim of her summer hat; I instantly felt lighter.

That afternoon, watched by Francoise's cool maternal

gaze, Georgina and I reclaimed The Fountains. We played tennis on the mossy and overgrown court with battered rackets, ducking and diving over the drooping net and blasting winning shots into the overgrowth of trees that surrounded it. We found abandoned chalets at the end of the grounds, filled with decaying newspapers left by the previous owner, which Francoise had doubtless been too laconic to remove. As we circled a forgotten tree house in a wooded copse Georgina notes that 'Francoise has probably never even bothered to walk through the grounds. She would have seen a few charming photos of it, in a carefully designed flier, and fallen in love with the hallway'. I had to concede that she was probably right.

The Fountains had its own voice that seemed to breathe from every corner. The more overgrown and neglected it revealed itself to be, the more that voice grew pronounced, steady and assuring. The Fountains was full of secrets, and however hard we tried to see every corner of it, it became increasingly apparent that it was too ephemeral a place to cover. As our time there progressed, more and more of it was alluded to until it seemed bigger than any of us. I would think we had seen every inch of it, just to find out about another corner essential to its essence. Like the feeling of success it evoked, The Fountains was a place where timeless resonance was taken for granted.

Francoise's butler had been looking for us for half an hour before he was able to call us inside to dress for dinner. Georgina and I had taken the iced tea Francoise had offered and lain by an empty swimming pool at the foot of the garden. In the afternoon sun the walls of the pool were coloured by precise maps of algae. Nonetheless, Georgina found it charming and she insisted that we unbutton our shirts and lay on our backs beside it. We looked up at the clouds and played our favourite childhood game, trying to find random shapes within each of them. At first I had resisted relaxing there, thinking there was something tragic and uneasy about the pool.

The same feeling returned to me as Georgina led me into the garden, which was this time cloaked in darkness. I couldn't help feeling uncertain about entering it at night, even following someone that I knew as intimately as her.

Georgina lifts her dress as she steps a few paces in front of me. As we draw nearer I see that each of the seven sculptures have been made to depict one of The Intimates.

"Have you seen this?" she asks. "Only Francoise would think of doing something like this for her guests. Which one is supposed to be me?"

The iced version of James clenches a paint brush, every limb of his elongated to the point of caricature, making him seem made purely of sinew and muscle. The sculpture of Barbara is pressing her hand to the skin above her bosom, her mouth open wide in rapture, as if she is embracing the adulation of an audience. Georgina stares directly into the face of her mothers sculpture. "No, still nothing behind the eyes."

We weave in and out of the silver steam emanating from each precisely chiselled form, Georgina posing and laughing as she loops her arm through Francoise's model, a picture of Gallic poise, taller than the rest.

Graham's statue holds aloft two surgical knives, and appears ready to plummet them back into the prostrate torso of some invisible patient. "Here you are, looking rather handsome, but a little short." My sculpture has a Kenneth Williams-like look of camp disgust on his face. "I think you're being aloof in this one," Georgina says, walking towards the statue of herself.

"I don't have a profession I could be attached to, hence the lack of props," I offer. The model of Georgina stands on the end, clutching what appears to be a wilting bunch of flowers under one arm, holding one out rather desperately. There appears to be a rather pleading look upon her face.

"There I am, touting whatever wares I can give away. Look, there's the summer house."

At the end of the lawn, only just visible amongst the vegetation covering its decaying façade, is the summer house. Georgina steps towards it, abandoning her heels in the spectral grass that's illuminated by the light from the house. "I can't believe it's still here," she says, moving to the swings next to it, which I remember her favouring during summer parties. I join her as she slips into one of the seats.

"Do you remember us being unsure about Francoise at first, until we had that party here during the first year?" I ask her.

"I was more uncertain of her than anyone. But at that party she seemed to treat us as though we were the people we one day would be, rather than the snotty students we actually were. There was something insightful about her, and it made me warm to her a little more."

"I remember her offering expensive bottles of champagne, and us spilling them onto one another on the lawn as we didn't know how to open them. I also remember you and I accidently smashing one of her windows during a game of tennis. But she just waved her hand nonchalantly and said, 'Try to take out one of the top ones. That would really impress me.'"

"Yes – I remember that. All of us lounging about on the grass in our tight fitting school sports gear, drinking champagne from teacups. And the whole time, me looking so suspiciously at her."

"I remember *that*," I laugh.

"I felt she lacked the history the rest of us had. And then I realised during the party that this summer house was an exact copy of the one your mother had made for us as children. It seemed a sign – that perhaps we should allow her into our gang."

"I remember my mum designing that summer house on a napkin during a garden party, when she couldn't bear to speak to any of the other adults there. I was sitting on her lap and telling her to add more turrets to it, and I remember thinking that my father would never allow it to be made. I was wrong – but then she always was the only one able to convince him to do anything."

"Your mum was the only parent who would ever play with us children. You remember that time we all went away to the lakes, don't you? Your family, my family, Carina and James' family. Your mum was the only one who spent more time with the children than discussing politics with the elders."

"I don't blame her for wanting to stay away from them that summer."

"I know. That was the summer they all decided to take a firm hand with our lives, wasn't it? We didn't know at the time what all those discussions were about, but when we went back to our usual lives we soon found out. They'd agreed to make all of us into child prodigies. I think those discussions cost each of us a rather large portion of our childhoods."

"My mum was the only one who voiced dissent at that agreement. Who said that it was ridiculous to expect little children to be brilliant when they were only just finding their feet. And after that the other parents shut her out. She was so different to all of the other parents there, she was a *mother*. When my father used to rage at me for being lost in a daydream, she used to tell him that it was a good thing, a sign that I would be as creative as him. But he used to hate hearing that. He always said a man should be focused, pragmatic. That she was far too soft on me, and when she died I think he felt that he now had the chance to compensate for how much I'd been indulged. He became even *more* forthright in his opinions of me. I'm sure he felt a keen sense of responsibility to her, to put me on the right path, even if it was not how she would have done it.

"She never pushed me; she wanted to leave me the space to find my own way. When she passed away there was no longer someone telling me that it was alright to feel as lost as this, that one day I would find my place in the world. That I didn't have to carry this enormous burden on my shoulders; that everything would eventually work itself out. I've tried so hard to remember her voice, but over the years it has gradually faded into the past. Always drowned out by louder voices, voices less distinct than hers."

"She was a wonderful woman Vincent. A single voice of sanity, particularly during that holiday. There was a lot going on behind the scenes that summer, wasn't there?"

"There was. I won't forget that in a hurry. That was the holiday when your mum fell out spectacularly with my Dad, and the atmosphere – "

"It was awful. I remember thinking that this must be what a divorce feels like – they were just so bitter and hateful towards each other. What was so sad about it was that the two of them went back further than anyone, they are the reason our little group actually exists today. Your mum acted in the first play he ever wrote, didn't she? And yet on that holiday your mum was so scared of him – hysterically, ridiculously scared. And all the parents took sides, and had to fall into one camp or the other. The start of that summer was all about diving in rivers, learning to catch fish, making snorkels out of the hollow branches of trees. The other half was like being on a daytime chat show."

"I don't think all our parents ever sat down at the same table again after that holiday."

"What was their argument even about?"

She swings for a minute, reaching down to brush a streak of mud from her naked leg as she points her toes at the house, straining to make the swing go higher. "Do you not remember? Did you not work it out?"

"There wasn't anything to work out," I answer. "They never told us anything, we were just kids."

"Did you not do any detective work? Were you really that wrapped up in your little action figures Vincent?"

"What did you find out?" I counter, stopping the swing and watching her pass me by, before she slows and eases herself to my side. "I thought it was just some needless argument that got out of hand."

"No, it wasn't that. My mother tried to seduce your father. At least, that's what I heard. I listened in at the parents' chalet, during one of those long drawn out arguments. A lot of the terms I heard at the time I didn't understand, but I thought about it again only the other day. I think your parents' marriage might have been going through a rough patch, and my mum of course saw an opportunity and pounced. And being my mother, she did not take rejection well. We all know your father's temper, and how quickly things escalated after that."

"I never knew."

"That surprises me. But then it shouldn't, knowing you as well as I do. You were so lost in your own world back then. Anything in reality that could possibly cause you pain just made you retreat. You had an imagination more fertile than any other child I knew."

"I remember those arguments. I remember my Dad detailing, with absolute precision, some of the things your mother shouted at him that summer. It amazes me that we are still friends, given what happened next."

"Yes, your father was pretty brutal."

I pull the swing back, before throwing my body towards the house on it. The silhouettes on the balcony are gold shapes passing amongst each other, floating inches above the lights on the pond. The figures look angelic, as if they're from a world separate to ours. I feel as though I am watching them in a film.

"I don't think we'd still be friends were it not for this little tribe of ours. It was them that insisted we remain close."

"They even tried to match make the two of us at one point, didn't they? Graham in particular was always saying, 'Think what a gesture it would be to both of your parents, to all of our parents, if the two of you started to date'. I can almost picture him rubbing his hands together as he said it. It's a shame we never did learn how to be in love with one another."

"I know," I say, smiling. She looks at me for a second, the twist of her mouth suggesting faint amusement, before she transfers her attentions to her feet. "They couldn't bear to see us fall out, could they? Graham was always reminding me during those early days, when we found we were in the same halls at university, of how the three of us had once put on little theatre productions in your garden."

"We were acting out your plays, little Vincent, don't you remember? You must have had some affection for your father then, because you were determined to be the little playwright of our group."

"It wasn't affection; it was a sense of competition. It makes me cringe to think. What plays did I write – the adventures of Robin Hood and Maid Marian, episodes 1-14? With you as Marian every time, no doubt."

"Sometimes Graham was Marian, Vincent. Those days were just wonderful, I remember them well. I loved acting out the lines you'd written, they seemed to always have a seam of magic running through them. Your mind was so agile, so alive. Even in our makeshift little theatre, made from cardboard boxes and abandoned slates of woodchip, I felt like a little star. I remember wanting to stay being the characters you'd written, wanting to embody those damsels in distress and live out every feature of their lives. My love for theatre came from those early plays of yours Vincent, there's no doubt about it."

"I like to think that you still have a love of theatre, that is hasn't been entirely lost."

"I'd like to say the same thing," she says, leaning against the chain of her swing. "The moment I was old enough she put me into auditions – for amateur productions and then for competitions as well, some at the other end of the country. Trying to make me into a little starlet. Her career had ended with a definitive slam of the door, and after a period convalescence she was funnelling all of that ambition, all of that hunger, into this little girl who was still unable to ride a bike."

"I remember. That haunted look in your eyes, with you always falling pale at the thought of not winning the next rosette for your mother."

"And the pressure built. I'd win one rosette, and the school would applaud me in assembly, and though I'd blush as I got up to collect it, inside I would feel magnificent. I thought I'd learnt what real happiness felt like – it was seeing the colour in her cheeks when I came off the stage after a victory, when she picked me up and swung me around her.

"But then I made some mistakes. I came second and third a few times, and initially though her encouragement remained, her optimism began to dim. And then one day, after months of feeling drawn and weak, I messed up the opening lines of a piece in a regional competition. She'd brought my grandma along to watch me, wheeled her out of her home for the first time in centuries, and I blew it spectacularly.

"I'll never forget the feeling – looking out into the audience as the judges condescendingly gazed down on this over-made up girl in a frilly dress. I felt utterly naked for a second, and then I sought my mum's eyes in the audience, to see that there was someone in the crowd for whom this failure didn't matter. And she looked so – utterly – humiliated. She didn't *speak* to me on the way home. Despite the vague qualifications of my grandma – who was too generous to care and too old to have any critical understanding. I remember her pulling me out of the car and practically throwing me towards the house. 'I'm so ashamed of you,' she said. 'That wasn't what we practiced at all.' And I cried and cried, and she didn't relent. And when the crying finally ceased, I came to my senses and for the first time I saw beyond her. And I've never seen acting in the same way since."

We swing for a minute, in utter silence. Only the sound of the chains rubbing against each other fill the air, and

describing us as 'the two creatures sucking the life out of me'. That diary helped me understand something about my mother that had always seemed inexplicable to me. I realised that she was unable to consider any situation from a perspective other than her own. We were only a week old when she decided that she needed space from us. That she needed 'the room to find success again'. I just couldn't really believe what I was reading.

"When I was a girl she never talked about the period of time when I was born, and it was only years later that I learnt anything about that time from her boyfriend. He told me that for the first few weeks we'd been looked after by a young Belgian nurse. As I grew up I began to suspect that perhaps *she'd* been somehow responsible for my brother's death. But this diary gave me a whole new take on that. Just before we were born she wrote about how much she wanted someone to look after us full-time, and she mentioned this Belgian girl, Annick, which a friend of hers at the local theatre had recommended. But the diary mentioned that she wasn't a nurse at all, but an au pair who had once, for a short while, performed the duties of a babysitter to give her friend the opportunity to go on tour. In the diary she wondered if Annick might offer a cheap solution to her predicament. She managed to contact her, and despite the fact that Annick was about to return to Belgium to find work, she convinced her to act as our carer until she 'got back on her feet'. But one afternoon a few weeks later, my left brother was left unattended in the bath, and he drowned. For years I wondered if Annick had simply been too inexperienced to handle two newborn babies. This diary finally answered that question for me.

"But I can't even think about that issue tonight. This party, for me, has one purpose. I want her to spend some time with The Intimates, to see how much our lives were affected by the little arrangement made by our parents that summer."

A bell rings from the house, and I sense a commotion taking place within it. A few moments later the shape of Francoise's butler appears at the top of the garden, stopping for a moment before making his way over to us. "Francoise must be about to read from her book," Georgina says.

In our absence the house has become a riot of music and laughter. Elise looks intrigued by my return, and as I feel her arm snake around my waist I notice a new wooziness in her movements. The guests are draped around various corners of the drawing room. Graham, caustic and mock-indignant, is holding court over Carina and Barbara, who are rapidly becoming hysterical. Franz is lying on his back on a couch at Francoise's side, as she rather nervously leafs through her slim volume. He strums a few chords for her, and she turns her face towards him. "I don't need musical backing on this one Franz," she says, and catches a butler's attention with her hand. "Walter, if Franz starts trying to distract me with flamenco chords during this reading, will you confiscate his guitar?"

Graham joins me at my side, offering me a glass. "I'm not alone in being terrified by all this, am I?"

"This must be so strange for you both," Elise says. "How old were you when this book was started?"

"You're about to see your boyfriend as he was during his flea-bitten student years," Graham says. "I hope Francoise will be gentle with us."

"I'm sure nothing that she says about you can surprise me too much," Elise says.

"Is this what being an author is going to be like?" Francoise asks her audience, quietening the clamour around her. "This is actually quite nerve-wracking."

She looks around for her glass of wine. For once her pristine demeanour is slightly ruffled – I'm seeing a side to her that I'm not used to.

"You should try getting a *real* job," Graham calls. Everyone laughs.

"Don't interrupt me when I'm working Graham," Francoise says, with an incisive smile.

"It's not surgery though, is it?" Graham replies, without missing a beat.

"We'll see," she answers, to a rising laugh. She turns to the front of her book, leaning against the piano at her side as she prepares to read. "Here we go."

'For some reason I feel quite vulnerable this evening. Though quite why I do is utterly beyond me. I have become accustomed to feeling invigorated by my new talented and youthful friends, and in return I believe that I offer them a little steadiness. This steadiness can only be earned, let alone passed on, after a few years amongst the shameless indifference of the world. Perhaps my nerves are borne out of nothing more than trepidation – as tonight is Franz's first performance. For so long he has played the role of mentor – particularly to Vincent and

Graham. But tonight his talents for the first time will yield a critical response.

'Over the course of the term he has put together a band of like-minded musicians, each of whom have been as seduced by his work as we are. I feel hopeful that these carefully nurtured songs will meet with a receptive audience tonight. But above all the prospect excites me – as carved within these songs are the personalities of each of The Intimates. They've encouraged and inspired their development, they feature copiously in their lyrics, and their insights form the backdrop to his current state of mind. The songs are marvellous, and out of all of us it is Franz, I feel, whose talents will find an international stage.

'A few years older than most of them, he is clearly the man Vincent hopes to emulate. Where Vincent is uncertain and mercurial, Franz is quietly assured and consistently creative. While Franz has developed his own unique style of Eastern Bloc chic, Vincent follows the fashions of the day however badly they match his own idiosyncrasies. Although I have never seen Franz perform, something tells me that tonight I will witness him fully expressing his own individuality, as he often does towards the end of parties, when he's at his most drunken and laconic. Vincent, no doubt, will be taking notes.

'Before we leave for the venue the seven of us agree to congregate at my flat, in the traditional way that every Friday night now begins. Rock 'n' roll chic is not a part of my fashion repertoire, and I struggle to make it so for one night. I leave my jewellery on the dresser, and seriously consider wearing some distressed jeans. But then Georgina arrives, wearing overly bright red lipstick and coiffed hair, and she tells me that I look like I am about to do some gardening. I relent, and wear an evening dress, and resolve that I will sit at the back. I have heard the music of her generation – it involves empty platitudes, nausea, and sonorous keyboards. It involves flat vocals and pale, wan faces. I know that the physicality of this concert will be nothing to be afraid of.

'Graham has interpreted the evening's dress code with a flamboyant determination. He has stolen a pair of Carina's fishnet tights, which are barely wide enough to accommodate a child's leg, and he is wearing one on each arm. His torso is covered with what appears to be a pillow case slashed with three long cuts, but which is in fact, a New Romantic vest. He's wearing leggings and has large swathes of rouge on each cheek. When he arrives he greets me as though this attire is entirely usual, and not at all a departure from his customary preppy aesthetic. I try to go along with this, and resist the urge to laugh at him. He looks like a boy who's fallen asleep with his head in his mothers' makeup bag (Graham laughs at this) and he doesn't quite have the physique to pull off his slim-fitting attire (his laughter subsides). I am meticulous in greeting him warmly. Carina laughs hysterically at him, and for some time. She has sculpted her hair into a quiff, and her cheeks for once hold some hint of colour. I suspect we are seeing her at her most unbridled.

'As James makes his way to the drinks cabinet I notice that his minor concession to contemporary style is to unbutton the very top of his shirt and not polish his shoes this evening. While the other guests arrive, as usual, he makes his way to the glass chess set that I keep in the living room. He consoles himself, like an errant child returning to his favourite corner, by playing out some historic end game on his own. James last year narrowly missed out upon becoming a young national chess champion, though his prodigious talents do not end there. He has recently begun to paint, and already local collectors have shown an interest in exhibiting his vivid, confrontational works. He has an intensity that I increasingly find promising, however uncomfortable it sometimes can be. I find his unyielding sincerity to be often misplaced, and at times a little dangerous. After a few drinks he can be formidable and witty, but he soon withdraws again into a twitchy state of introversion. I fear his analytical way of thinking makes him interpret the world as a series of contracts. He is yet to understand the insincerity of a world which fuels itself on empty platitudes and meaningless statements. He denotes semantic reason behind every statement, and I fear one day he will feel maligned by someone's empty promises unless he learns to abandon this tendency.

'Carina creates excellent Bloody Marys for each of us. Her cocktails are marvellous, though not even I can quite handle them. As we wait for the others to arrive she dances with me, and I again feel maternal towards her. She has such understated beauty, such untapped potential. If she learns to become conscious of her attractiveness she will realise how it can labour on her behalf. At present she is shy; some may even find her reticence rather flat. She reproduces every mannerism I make, and I feel quite flattered by her attention. She is increasingly nourished by the assurance that our little group offers her. She mentioned that she's considering dropping her studies and focusing purely on her ballet for the remainder of her university years. Although hugely encouraged when I urged her to do so, I sensed she is still frightened of her father's disapproval should she sway from his chosen path. She has not yet found that sacred middle ground which I sought too cautiously – of living the life you want while gently placating your elders. I must dedicate some time towards encouraging her to grasp this necessary opportunity.

'Georgina bustles in from practice still wearing the clothes from her dress rehearsal, with her cheeks rouged like an eighteenth century moll. In moments she is throwing back Bloody Marys, dancing with us to the gramophone and announcing her relief that the weekend has begun. She has just been offered the lead part in the university's summer revue, a remarkable achievement considering it was her first acting audition since childhood. I'm told that the directors were quite startled by her raw ability. She has thrown herself into this role with the fervour of the recently converted. I am so pleased – she seemed lost and conflicted when we first met, and now she seems inspired. When Carina asks her how the rehearsal was she is positively queenly in her response, which is just adorable. I can sense already her mother's acute sense of self-worth now she has started to act. I can only hope this does not develop with too great a sense of entitlement, though I suspect we are seeing some understandable feelings of vindication expressed now. When she talks of how nervous the other actresses are, there's a sympathy in her voice that suggests she is wary of being swept up in the glamour of it all. I'm sure she's very aware of how the movie industry burnt her mother, and mindful that she must preserve her love of acting without allowing any attendant flames to scorch her.

'We drink shots, and Graham performs some spontaneous comedy turn for us all as the evening officially begins. He seems more comfortable than usual in his feminine attire, as if outlandish outfits allow him to feel at last as if he is himself. He insists on inviting my elderly neighbours in for drinks, who he spies in the hallway. I ache with sympathy when I see the old dears sipping vodka as if it's a mildly brewed tea that has been left to grow inexplicably cold. The sight of this elderly couple being offered tequila by a man wearing fishnet tights on his arms is quite memorable. This new image seems at odds with the Graham we are familiar with; a man whose first year medical exam results were the highest in the country. He is one of the few in our group whose personal constitution seems unlikely to hold him back.

'Vincent arrives just as the rest of us are becoming inebriated, just as we are due to leave. Carina, I notice, has refrained from drinking too much. She lacks the confidence to throw herself into proceedings and allow her demeanour to be threatened by spontaneity. But I wonder if she also restrains herself because she wishes to be preserved for Vincent's arrival. Though they barely nod at one another in greeting, they spend the rest of the night at each other's side. When one of them is distracted they are followed keenly by the other's gaze, which promptly snaps away on their return. There seems to be a strange symmetry in their mutual attraction. As I am increasingly fascinated by Vincent's father's work, so my protégé is increasingly drawn to his son. It's not just their stolen glances which make me believe they are destined for one another, it's the peculiar uncertainties they share. Neither of them seems assured enough to make the first move, to threaten their own pride for long enough to clumsily reach for happiness. I hope it is not a tendency that will plague either of their lives. Soon, when they realise the brevity of this paltry and prescribed existence, I am sure one of them will clear their throat and make a proposal. Until then, they must continue this ridiculous dance, ignoring those whose company they never leave.'

I notice Elise draw away from me, biting her bottom lip. "Are you alright?" I ask, and she nods, not meeting my eye. I see her search for some kind of reaction in Carina. But Carina's expression is vacant; she glances over at me with a slightly amused smile, as if she is being teased. I notice she is blushing. The reaction flatters me, and I look away to disguise it. James considers me with a reproaching and disappointed expression. Francoise looks up and carefully registers these reactions. A little falteringly, she returns to the page.

'There's barely room to breathe, let alone move at the concert, and I am delighted this is the case. Vincent hurries to his guru, practically begs him to see if there is anything he can do, but Franz has everything in hand. The room seems filled with all the most important faces, and Franz moves comfortably amongst them. He is yet to play a note, and yet I can see the transference of these skills to the international stage will be a seamless, elegant gesture, performed with a transfixing sense of inevitability.

'Before Franz takes to the stage I see Vincent moving lovingly amongst the instruments, as if by merely being on stage he is worshipping at a shrine. Vincent has a voracious hunger to express himself and find reward through the act, so much so that I am frightened he will now look to music for the answers to his questions. Frightened, because Vincent takes to new causes with excessive zeal, but is too vulnerable to accommodate criticism. I know already that Vincent has no musical talents, and that his gifts lay elsewhere. And yet something tells me that all of us will have to see him play through the motions of walking exactly in Franz's footsteps, and none of us will dare say a discouraging word. Vincent's enthusiasm, his interest in everything and his need to consume will stand him in good stead. But we are all aware of how sulky and introverted he can be if his little experiments are criticized. He is a curious mixture of assurance and vulnerability, and I hope that inevitable tests to his confidence will not dent his bravado. The link between these two traits is self-centredness, yet he cares keenly about his friends and so is developing as a man of intriguing contradictions. The uncomfortable truth is that he has a talent very similar to his father's. He has recently distributed a promising manuscript amongst our group; an excerpt from it won a prestigious regional literary award. I fear that he will only belatedly realise that his talents lie in this area.

'The concert is a triumph. Franz electrifies the audience with his teasing, emotive songs, with the addictive growl of his voice, with the glacial quality of his instrumentals. His choruses embed themselves in the ear, so that a few are mouthing along to the words even as the songs begin to end. His bandmates, in their black uniforms, look to him for affirmation and leadership. They play a thrilling encore, which has the venue moving as one and roaring for more, and when he takes to the stage alone, for an acoustic encore, his words of gratitude are self-effacing and charming. He looks every inch the lizard-like rock star, baring his soul and basking in the sheer warmth that emanates from the audience. It is exactly as I imagined a good rock concert to be – visceral, life affirming, and yet with enough meaning to make one more spontaneous than they had previously dared to be.'

Francoise gives a small smile, and her little audience applaud and cheer kindly. She hands the volume to her butler, and says, "Thank you. I was quite nervous, and your approval is most kind. I hope my small observations were received as generously as your applause was given. Back then I was a star-struck and occasionally inspired little girl, so don't take anything I said too seriously."

"It was very interesting," Elise says, as Francoise comes over.

Francoise registers the look of concern on my face. "Oh my dear, you must ignore what I said about Vincent and Carina; they were just children at the time. So much has changed since then."

"And yet your predictions were confident enough to give us a time scale," James notes.

"James, if he was attracted to Carina something would have happened by now," Francoise says, looking absently over our shoulders. My eyes meet Carina's for a second; she is gesturing towards Francoise. Francoise excuses herself to speak with her.

"A little close to the bone, wasn't it?" Graham says, pouring Elise a drink. "I was dressed up that night as a show of support to Franz, I remember it quite specifically. It wasn't that I felt I had *found my look*."

"As she says, she was just a girl when she wrote it. The importance of the piece is that it reminds us of that time, of how we related to one another as teenagers. She isn't trying to make a point that's any bigger than that," I counter.

"You think so? That was a long book, and I find it interesting that Francoise chose to read such a confrontational section from it. She seems keen to make the seven of us look in the mirror, and yet she's careful to avoid any scrutiny herself."

"I think some of her observations sailed pretty close to the wind," Elise says. "I kept looking over to Barbara, to see if any of those comments smarted, but she seemed pretty oblivious to them."

"Barbara's defences are well constructed, she would have to work a lot harder than that to find a chink in them," Graham says. "I say that when we team up for the party game later we turn the tables on Francoise a bit, let her feel a little heat from us. What do you think?"

Elise's face lights up.

"I think you are a vindictive tranny with bricks in her handbag," I say. Graham laughs. "Don't be too hard on her."

"She's a big girl," Graham answers, turning away. "She can take it."

A few minutes later James is ruffling through a book as we seek temporary solace in the library. I watch the veins in his long hands tighten as he impatiently flips pages under the delicate light. The chandelier has been inactive for many years, but this evening he has blinked it back to life, and it seems to shroud him in a grateful glow. He's trying to find a passage he wants to read to me, something from a book we both read at university, but I don't feel brave enough to tell him that it doesn't matter. I glance upwards, bewildered by the endless row of books.

"These were inherited by her," he says, smiling in my direction. "She occasionally passes through here and picks over a Baudelaire, in a vague attempt to feel intellectual." I lean against a dusty stack. The memories feel a little woozier now, disturbed by the wine I gradually drank during the reading. My earlier remembrances were bright, pin sharp, but now they are smeared with fragrances and lights.

"Art is so often wasted isn't it?" James says, more to himself than to me. "People seem comforted to see books in plush libraries, but what use are they if no-one ever bothers to read them? Fields of consideration, laid out in detail, to gather dust, to rot." He snaps the book shut. "Are you still writing?"

Not as much as I should. "Yes. At university it was a guilty pleasure to write, as I felt I should be concerned with something loftier. Now I don't write as I feel I shouldn't be concerned with something that lofty."

He runs a long finger down a weathered page, before dismissing it and transferring his attention to another volume. "It's a paradox," he says. "The work we make in our youth is too pure to be considered serious, but when we are old enough to be deemed worthy of attention we are too serious to be pure. You shouldn't dismiss those adolescent musings of yours. If they're shaped with the discipline of maturity they may yet reveal themselves as unpolished jewels." He somehow makes the prospect seem ugly.

I don't respond, and he turns to face me. "I remember the manuscripts you used to write at university. And if I remember rightly they were completely unselfconscious, so untainted by worldliness. Their insights were very acute."

I don't know if I should thank him, but feel frightened to risk an emotional reaction if I do. As he looks up, smiling, I recoil a little as his gaze meets mine. His eyes appear covered in a thick white paste. It's unsettling to remember that the man who's leafing through these books struggles to read a word of them.

"Forgot didn't you?" he whispers, smiling with the corners of his mouth. He looks right at me, and I struggle to connect his words as my eyes fix upon the white sheen. "People always forget. They assume I'm *normal*."

"You are normal. It's just that I temporarily forgot."

"I never have that luxury. We were talking about the past," he says, his leafing starting afresh. "Reminding me of the boy I was then. Useful, vigorous. Blessed with focus."

"I've seen your recent work. In many ways they possess more focus than your earliest paintings."

"If I hadn't known you as long, that comment could have caused great offence," he says, with a gradual, sickly smile. As his head tips back to consider a new row it is garishly lit by the light above him. I notice his skin is starting to perspire, that the sharp cut of his profile has remained unchanged over the years. That slightly keen, flattened forehead, on top of an overlong body. As I glance at him again I imagine him, pale and impassioned, clattering amongst paint pots in his frozen house.

"Do you have any writing that I'm yet to see then Vincent?"

I feel somehow threatened by this recourse to my past. "There is this one piece," I say. "But I haven't been able to recapture the urgency with which I started it at university. The more I add to it, the more I let it cool." I realise I am reflecting the patterns of his speech now, the halting, forced rhythms of his words. "The newspaper has me on standby through the week, so it's hard to lose myself in any new work."

"You wanted to write novels originally, didn't you? Both of us seem to have ended up compromising a little. Not achieving what we set out to? Both of us must be familiar with that clammy, indulgent grief then."

I nod, wanting to agree more, but wonder if pursuing a connection with him is such a good idea. "I wonder how I'll deal with it as it gets worse. Because it will."

There is something otherworldly about him; he appears so pale and drawn as he flickers through books he can hardly read. For a moment I wonder if he is a figment of my imagination. I feel a compulsion to leave, but don't want to appear rude. There's also something compelling about the way he relentlessly flips through every book on the shelf. The obsessive manner in which he considers each in turn, looking for a brief passage we once discussed in our twenties, is ridiculous and yet entrancing. Though I feel a distinct urge to leave him, one that's almost impossible to quell, I'm also intrigued to find out what he wants from me.

"I can read you know," he says, snapping his gaze at me. "I'm not *blind*." He spits the word out. "Cerebral achromatopsia, that's what it's called. I see everything in grey." I wonder if I should finish my glass. I catch a view of him from the side, wondering if he knows. What a terrible affliction for an artist. How did –

"You're wondering how it happened, aren't you?" he says, turning to me with those pale eyes, before pronouncing each word as though he's said them a thousand times.

"How on earth do you know that?"

He straightens a little, as if offended by my directness. "It's not difficult to work out. A period of silence, as you leant slightly into my body. With my condition you learn to pick up what a normal person ignores. You've forgotten what happened, haven't you? The drink again, is it?"

"Perhaps."

"It involves Carina. Ring any bells?"

"Yes," I say, keen for him to not dwell on it, to not become angry. "I remember now."

"I've always wanted to know your take on the whole affair."

"Affair?"

"You know what I mean," he snaps. "This party, tonight, it's brought it all up for me again. I want to know how you feel about her role in what happened."

"It isn't really any of my business James."

"We *are* Intimates," he says, as if hissing some meaningful password at me. "Which means that everything that's happened between her and I *is* your business. You are pretending to have forgotten; let me remind you." The book is back on the shelf now, and I can't help but look away from his confrontational pose. To my glass, to the floor. To anywhere.

"A few years after university she and I fell out of touch. It was very strange, as we were so close in our youth. I called round her house one night, rather late, though she had been a little unclear about whether or not she would be in. A man was there. Fine, I thought, she is enjoying the company of a friend." I feel myself straighten up.

"She knew that I might be coming over that night Vincent, which is what was so strange. And when she answered the door – I admit I had been drinking a little – she expressed extreme surprise at seeing me there. 'I telephoned earlier,' I said. 'Do you not remember? We agreed it would be lovely to meet up again. They were your words.' 'Oh, of course,' she said, smiling gaily. 'I remember.' And then I went inside and there, by the fireplace, was this swarthy Latino man, you know the type she attracts. Antoine, or something. 'Good evening James,' he says, mocking me, you know. 'What is this?' I ask her. She looks embarrassed. Pretends to be caught in the act. I storm outside, not knowing whether to stay and clock him or to pull her outside to get to the bottom of it. And she follows me into the drive. 'Carina,' I plead. 'You know how I feel about you. How I've always felt about you. I'm in love with you, and that's never going to the change. If you've invited your little toy boy over to tease me then you are not the woman I thought you were.'

"'It's not that,' she said, suddenly becoming articulate for the first time in years. 'You know I'm fond of you James, but you have always just been a dear friend of mine. I would never have invited Antoine here to embarrass you. I just wasn't aware that you were definitely coming over, that's all.'

"'Embarrass me?' I answered. I was flinching at this point. 'Embarrass *me*? It's you who should be embarrassed, playing these sick little games. You've strung me along for years and I've crawled around on the ground after you like some love-sick puppet. Because that is what I have been, love sick.'

"'Please James,' she said. 'Please calm down, come in for a drink.'

"'For a drink? With your disgusting little man toy? You really are a repulsive little creature,' I said, and I leapt back into the car."

"You had an accident that night, didn't you James," I say, trying to hurry him before he gets even more emotional.

"That's an understatement, my boy. A real understatement. I was angry, out of my mind. You can imagine. She'd pushed me to my limit, and then nudged me off the edge. 'Come in for a drink?' Can you imagine the neck of that woman?" I try to remain looking passive.

"Yes, I'd had a drink, but it was the anger that did it. I was a man who'd lost his grip. We all have limits, Vincent. I sped into the night, and three minutes later came off a sharp corner, obscured by poplar trees. Boom, straight off the cliff. Then I got this," he flips his hands up at his eyes. "And was faced with staring into a grey tunnel for eternity."

The sound of music from the drawing room reaches my ears and I'm inclined to follow it, but something makes me stay. "I can only see in darker shades of grey now," he whispers, taking my arm. I can smell the sweat on his shirt, the mustiness of his breath. In one precise movement he places the slim book back into the exact slot he drew it from, without even looking up. Even with twenty-twenty vision it would be an impressive act, but in this half-light it really unsettles me. "At first it was just light and dark grey that I saw in. Now it's just various shades of sludge."

"It must have been devastating, for a painter... "

"You have no idea. My world revolved around colour, sensation. It was how I guided myself, how I was inspired. I felt my way through colours every day, and in one blinding second I had that centre point taken away from me. Had to stumble through everything, had to find some new niche. I guess what each colour is now, and have to rely on the clumsy compliments of strangers to determine the success of new paintings. Have you ever tried to eat a dish of something that's completely that colour?" I shake my head, guiltily. "Or tried to make love to a woman whose body looks just like clay?" His voice is rising now, slightly more emotional. "My early work was exhibited in Florence, Prague; there was talk of a New York exhibition. Reviewers said I would 'finish what Paul Klee started'. A cruel fate, isn't it?"

"I can't imagine – "

"No, you can't." The sound of Barbara's laughter reverberates through the aisles. It is hideously inappropriate. "And we know whose fault it is, don't we Vincent? That becomes increasingly clear, with every year that passes."

"Now come on James, you can't blame Carina for your accident."

"She wasn't in the car. It's not as if we were on some jolly together and she drove me off the road. But it was her that put me in that state of mind Vincent, it was. To be treated like that by a fellow Intimate? And even if you don't think she was to blame for the state of my vision, she must be accountable for more than that?"

"What do you mean?"

"Oh come on Vincent. I was in love with her. Desperately, hideously in love. And for years she strung me along and then rejected me, in the most humiliating way possible. In front of a man who is everything I am not. How damning a verdict upon me. She stripped me of my confidence, my potency. I haven't been in love since Vincent, and I never will again. She took away my sexuality, Carina did, she stole it from me."

"Is everything alright in here?"

Francoise suddenly appears at the end of the corridor, against a backdrop of bright gold light. She's holding two glasses of champagne, and she smiles kindly but firmly at us. "Ah, the hostess. Here to toast my ruin," James mutters. Francoise slides her slender arm through mine, and the room seems instantly warmer.

"You two must join the other guests," she admonishes, propelling the two of us towards the doorway. "I've decided that we are going to play a little party game."

Barbara is lingering at the entrance to the drawing room. Francoise pushes James towards her, amused perhaps by the potential contrast. "He's like the ghost of Christmas past, that man," she whispers, drawing close. "You look pale. He does that."

After the isolation of the library the drawing room is a blaze of colours. The scent of wine escapes everyone's lips; gold liquids bubble from glasses, foaming over slick fingers before being pressed to open, painted mouths. Smiles are flashed from person to person, erupting into laughter and then snapping away. Polished flesh, once carefully concealed, is now exposed and flushed excitedly with wine. Jazz music emanates from the gramophone, prompting the shoulders and feet of the guests to move in time with that urgent, incessant rhythm.

Carina uncoils her long dark hair, looking over as it bobs around her shoulders. Graham pulls off his bowtie, casting it behind him and moving forward. He draws a cigarette from his breast, lights it, and then places it between his lips, now pursed in expectation. Franz holds a violin bow in the corner of the room, excited and cautious. As Francoise enters the room she waltzes in time to the music, greeted by a rising cheer from her guests.

"You disappeared," Elise says, as I join her, Carina and Graham in a corner of the room.

"Tonight, we are on the same team," Graham says, placing his hand on my shoulder. "This is the moment when Francoise gets to feel the spotlight on *her*."

As Francoise acts out the film written on the card before her, her body moves with forced precision. She taps her arm to denote syllables, she plucks imaginary light bulbs from the ceiling, she pretends to delicately shop at a market stall as Georgina, Barbara and Franz shout film titles at her. "Barbara ought to be good at this – she did it for a living once," Graham whispers, Carina berating him with a gentle pat.

"How did you not work that out?" Francoise exclaims, as the buzzer snaps her mime to an end.

"How did you not find my spout?" Graham answers, pretending to not understand her accent.

"I'm not talking to you; you are not on my team," Francoise replies, trying not to smile.

"This is not a cuisine? Francoise, none of us can *understand* you when you've had a drink," Graham says. "If you're going to be the hostess and instruct us to play party games you must be sober enough to speak English properly."

"Your English is *parfait*, Francoise, ignore him," Barbara says.

"He's just trying to cause divisions within us because he knows his own team lacks talent," Georgina says.

"Excuse me, Elise is a dark horse. She showed me her impression of Francoise before she came in, and proved that she is a naturally gifted mimic," Graham retorts.

"I did not do an impression of you," Elise says to Francoise, but I can tell from the blush on her cheeks that she's lying.

James enters the room, clutching a glass of brandy, and Carina's eyes flash cautiously over to him. "Can you work out what Francoise is saying James?" Franz asks, looking up at him. "She is being too Parisian for any of us to understand."

Graham and I simultaneously guess Carina's film in seconds. Elise reacts as if smarted. Afterwards, Carina slips into her chair, closing her eyes as she draws out a cigarette.

"How did you know what film she was doing?" Elise asks.

"We watched that film together once at university," he says, looking between the two of us.

"Your go now Elise," Francoise commands, and as she rises to her feet I sense Elise willing herself to usurp Carina.

Carina reclines, pushing a slim plume of smoke from her lips and looking up as it dissolves around the chandelier above our heads. She barely bothers to watch as Elise frenetically acts, Graham and I firing film names at her until the alarm erupts, to jeers from Franz and Barbara. I feel guilty for being embarrassed by Elise's energy; she looks angry as she draws back towards us.

"I'm sorry," I say, as she moves to her seat, her cheeks more flushed than before. "It was *Dances With Wolves*," she snaps. "The first film that we watched together."

"Terrible of you not to have got that really," Graham says.

I feel Georgina's eyes trying to find mine as Franz loudly applauds Barbara's acting. Barbara performs a scene from one of her more successful films, bowing elaborately when Franz guesses it in seconds. "You can't just do any film you want!" Georgina exclaims. "You are supposed to pick a film at random from the bowl!"

"Nonsense," Barbara says, sitting as close to Franz as she reasonably can without straddling him. "That's not how the game works."

"It is, isn't it Francoise?" Georgina asks.

"Dissension in the ranks... can't you keep your team together?" Graham calls.

"You won't create civil war in us, our loyalties are unbreakable!" Franz jeers.

"Georgina," Francoise instructs. "It is your turn."

Franz sits back, conscious that he must not judge Georgina's acting superior to her mother's. The clock starts.

"I knew you couldn't do it," Barbara says, when the alarm eventually sounds. "She never could act," she whispers to Franz. Georgina stops and looks over at me, a look of humiliation playing on her face.

"That's hardly fair," James says, as Georgina passes wordlessly behind him.

"Carina, your turn. Franz, please make the music louder," Francoise orders, keen to extinguish the sudden and rather painful silence.

"I'm sure you'll manage to get this in seconds," Elise says, as Carina steps to her feet.

Carina dances drunkenly to the music for a few moments, as if steeling herself, before setting down her glass as the clock starts. For the full minute she holds the same pose, her arms held aloft as she moves her hips, as if slowly wading through treacle. Graham and I flounder for guesses, Elise retaining a determined silence until the alarm sounds. "I was trying to be Anita Ekburg in *La Dolce Vita*," she says, as she steps back behind Graham.

"Could you have been any less creative?" Graham asks, and Carina lifts two fingers up at him.

"I'm surprised you weren't a better actress," James whispers. "I'd have thought you'd be good at selling illusions."

"Graham might have been better suited to that part. It's his favourite film," I say, as Carina tucks a lock of hair slowly behind her ear.

I look over to the gramophone as the music starts to fade.

A hand reaches out and replaces the record with one that hums and crackles for a moment, before erupting into a galloping rhythm. The guests cheer loudly.

An Egyptian man in a white suit enters the room, acclaiming us with one hand as the lights go up. He is holding a long, elaborately decorated drum under one arm. A second, louder roar greets his accomplice, a belly dancer whose long body shimmers in gold and scarlet sequins as the butlers make space for her. In moments the man is drumming out a pulse-quickening tattoo that drowns out the gramophone. He bites his bottom lip and sweat builds on his forehead as the dancer shimmies to the front of him.

The drum is soon accompanied by enthusiastic clapping from the guests. The man's head is bowed, all of his concentration channelled into the wonderfully earthy sound of this drum, a lone instrument with which he seems to pummel the world into sense. I wonder if he isn't burrowing to find some essence that he himself has lost, some link to his past. Or if he is in fact tunnelling towards a more sensuous future by creating a canvas for this Turkish woman to move her hips over. It startles me that a man can commit such unbending passion to so simple an instrument. But the simplicity of the drum beat makes perfect sense as it inspires the bouquet of sensations the dancer provokes.

"It looks as though the party has taken a sordid turn," Elise says. "What is this, a Middle Eastern striptease?"

"It's a Raqs Sharqi belly dance, and this woman is one

of its most famous exponents," Carina says, in an awed voice.

"She looks like a lap dancer. Bit fat for it, isn't she?"

Carina looks at Elise as if confused. "She's amazing, watch what she can do."

The dancer swirls her hips in time to the building drum-beat, which seems keen to accelerate her into a state of abandon. But with a composed, warm smile the dancer resists the temptation, her searching fingers finding new texture in the brutal drumming. This ability to absorb a man's frantic passion and express it sensuously, defines the beauty of femininity, played out in a timeless dynamic before us.

Barbara hoists her glass into the air and mimics the dancer's movements. Fortunately the dancer seems oblivious to this, as if she is somewhere else entirely. Franz copies Barbara for a few moments, before craning a champagne bottle towards her. Liquid spills out of the bottle and into her glass in one long, foamy gesture. Barbara holds the glass above her head, hoisting her dress over her cleavage with the other hand. Francoise dances along with them, allowing James to cup her waist as he reluctantly joins the rest of the writhing bodies.

Carina's face is alight; her attention passing between the aggressive drums and the exotic way the dancer quells his fervour. "Isn't she wonderful? I wish I could dance like that."

"I heard that you're recovering well," Graham says, over the riot. "That you feel almost no pain now when you dance."

Carina's attention remains with the dancer, but a second later she considers Graham's voice. "I'm lucky that it doesn't hurt to walk anymore, and that it doesn't hurt at night. But whenever I dance, a piercing pain comes through me. I won't let it stop me though – dancers like her remind me that I mustn't give up." With these words I remember Carina's story. That just after she left university she was training as a dancer, on track for fame until a riding accident left her barely able to move.

"Perhaps inspiring you is what Francoise had in mind?" Graham suggests.

Franz steps over, his cheeks rosy with laughter and port. "If the band were here, I would convince them that we should persuade this temptress to dance in our next video."

"It's a shame you can no longer use the band to get a girl's number," Graham says.

"I agree," he replies. "A famous band name is like a successful brand, it's an advert for a certain lifestyle. The band name opened many doors to me, but now I have to rely upon more temperamental gifts – like charm and money, which increasingly diminish with time." He leans against a pillar and considers the dancer with a melancholy expression. "Women like this make me laugh at the shallowness of my youth. When we were famous I was interested only in chasing after models and hostesses, women who pleased my ego, who I thought were satisfied by limousines and champagne. I should have used my influence to travel to far flung lands, to learn about the exoticism of women of the earth like her, whose movements evoke cultures that I could only ever glimpse inside."

For the first time tonight I am now seeing the Franz that I once knew; who dispelled our fears and pushed each of us, blinking with expectation into the world.

"Do you not agree with me Vincent?" he says, wiping his brow. "Do you not see how we live superficial lives when we mock other cultures – by dismissing them with our consuming mindset?"

"I see that you should definitely drink less tequila," Graham replies.

"No, he is right," I say, suddenly inspired. "It relieves me to hear you talk like this again Franz. Femininity charms us, because it evokes a world that men have no access to. The entire range of female paraphernalia is so seductive; a glimpse of it is a glimpse into the machinery which creates illusions we lust and despair after for a lifetime. The furs, the perfume bottles, the lip gloss containers that illuminate the dresser; all are transformed from something mundane into something timeless with their mere application, and thereby provoke a thirst that can't be quenched. Women of the world inspire because they show how limited even that appreciation of women is; they prompt us to venture into the world so we can understand their essence and gain their charms."

Elise rolls her eyes. "So you're saying that you are only ambitious in order to gain the attention of foreign women?"

"No. The boy is hungry for the world, even if that hunger is sometimes only manifested through desire."

Franz smiles kindly at me.

"What does he know about desire, let alone women?" she retorts, more assertive now that a few eyes are upon her. "I could teach this belly dancing harlot a thing or two, and I wouldn't need to dress up like a tramp in order to do it. She's just a girl who's decorated herself as a woman."

Carina rises to fetch a drink. The remark seems to have stung her, perhaps given her earlier admittance that she felt she had not gained whatever is required to become a woman. For a moment I am compelled to seize her, to tell her to ignore Elise. To tell her that by confessing her own uncertainty Carina has simply made herself all the more difficult to define, and thereby all the more feminine. That Elise's need to define herself serves only to strip away some of her charm.

I watch Carina as she moves away. She skirts everyone carefully, keen to not draw attention to herself, or make anyone move on her account. Elise on the other hand, moves so that she is sat directly between Franz and I, her eyes flickering between the two of us to ensure that she still has our attention.

I wonder then if female beauty perhaps manifests itself in two ways. Women either decide to be beautiful, and with constant assertion of that decision become it, in many people's eyes. Or they decide they're beautiful but then live naturally in the shadow of that belief, with infinitely more charm. If this is the case, it seems Elise is the former type, and Carina the latter.

"I occasionally did some burlesque dancing when I was

at university," Elise says. "My performances were far more risqué than any of this belly dancing. Performing at a private party to an appreciative audience is nothing – I'd sometimes have to win over a roomful of men using nothing but a couple of tassels and a horsewhip."

Franz cocks his head appreciatively. "A horsewhip? Elise, are you suggesting there is a darker side to the innocent primary school veneer that we have all taken for granted?"

"Oh, I definitely have a darker side. One that even Vincent knows nothing about."

Elise flashes a look at me, perhaps trying to gauge my reaction. I smile, and try to look quietly intrigued. Being careful not to let on how this does not make her sound dark or decadent to me at all – merely desperate and a little unhinged.

"Are you going to show us some of your moves then?" Franz asks. She laughs coquettishly.

"She is a very good dancer," I say. "But I suspect you have not known these people long enough to dance for them Elise."

"Let the girl decide herself," Franz insists. "If she says she wants to dance, then dance she must. I think I'd rather like to see it."

"Are you worried that other men will see how desirable I am?" Elise asks, laughing and then kissing me on the cheek.

The dancer finishes to a chorus of cheers, before bowing with a final flourish. As I go to refill my glass Carina rushes over to speak with her. The dancer seems flattered by her praise, and she slowly takes Carina through a couple of her steps. Carina, with some trepidation, follows each of them with curious and grateful eyes. In minutes she has mastered a couple of her movements, and the dancer laughs encouragingly as Carina insists she repeats them for her. But as she moves away I see Carina clasp her hip and steady herself against a table, a look of disappointment quickly flashing in her eyes.

I feel tempted to rush over to her and console her. I want to compliment her for her determination to dance again, to assure her that in time she will be able to. But something stops me. That gradual paralysis which always inevitably affects me when I am around her.

"Quite the fare you have put on for your guests," Graham says, as Francoise joins us.

"I met the dancer when I was travelling through Egypt," she replies. "I promised to pay for her fare and accommodate her if she performed at our little soiree."

"I'm glad you invited me this evening," Elise says. "The Fountains really is a wonderful place to spend an evening."

"You are fortunate to be here on a night when all of The Intimates are together," Carina says. "It doesn't happen very often. Vincent must have told you a lot about our little group?"

"I have, yes."

"Have you?" Elise says. "You did say you were keen to see everyone again, but also that you've changed a lot since university. I thought you said you were concerned that it might be a little awkward?"

"I'm not sure I said that Elise. I've known these people for far too long to have any such concerns."

"I'm very glad you made it," Francoise says, to Elise. "I was intrigued to meet you, and you haven't disappointed. I'm pleased you are so taken with The Fountains. Many say that the whole estate is cursed, and it certainly has been a labour of love for me. But now I have it almost as I desire, and I have grown quite attached to it."

"Wasn't it owned by some wealthy aristocrat, who fell into squalor upon acquiring it?" Graham asks.

"You mustn't believe the villagers' gossip about this place. Some of it originates from me, so that I could lower the price. It is true that the original owner was very comfortably well off, until he lost his wife and much of his wealth in a freak series of events. He built The Fountains as a fresh start – the name itself obviously evokes visions of clear running water with which he hoped to wash away the debris of his past. In the grounds he placed three large and rather ornate fountains – one to symbolise the future, one for the past, and one for the present. He always intended that the fountain for the future would be the most powerful, to symbolise him overcoming the adversity that had blighted much of his life. Unfortunately for him, his new start was not as successful as he hoped it would be. Having lost most of his riches he disappeared into thin air one day – allowing me to purchase The Fountains at a steal. The villagers say that the grounds are cursed, that they eventually take a hold of their owner and ruin them.

I have worked hard to overcome that myth, for that is all I believe it to be. And I think I have been somewhat successful – as since residing in The Fountains I have finally published my long-awaited novel."

"You could never own a house without there being some spooky story behind it, could you Francoise?" Graham says. "I wonder if *all* these rumours do not begin and end with you. In fact, I would not put it past you to have made these rumours up, just so you could play a little game with your guests and see how we react to it all. The bored and rich have such wicked imaginations."

Francoise smiles weakly, and looks over at me. "Vincent, you don't believe I would act so callously, do you?"

"You might, to acquire a house like this."

"You must let me show you the house Vincent, there is so much of it that you have not seen. Perhaps if you see it for yourself, you will realise that none of its intrigue was applied by me. Elise, can I steal your boyfriend from you for a short while?"

"As long as you bring him back unchanged, yes."

Francoise holds the tips of my fingers as she leads me out of the drawing room, and I feel Elise's eyes on the back of my head as she does so. Something about Francoise's touch seems to heighten my awareness. I feel conscious I should be on my guard, and yet strangely excited by the thought of being alone with her. As I follow her I fall into the slipstream of her perfume, which combined with the drink makes me feel a little weak.

"Elise has a keen pair of eyes," Francoise says, looking back at me with a smile. "I wonder if she treats the world with such constant suspicion. It must wear her out."

"Our little group must be rather a lot for her to take in. I wonder if she isn't slightly envious of our shared past."

Francoise leads me through the library. We ease past stacks and stacks of undisturbed books, dusty and peaceful. Her eyes remain fixed upon the back wall until we draw up against it. "Bear with me," she whispers, casting her eyes along the top shelf until she fixes upon a battered copy of Ayn Rand's *The Fountainhead*.

"Walter, will you close the library door?" she calls, as she looks behind us.

"Certainly madam," the butler replies. The room quickly dims as he does so.

"Let me show you something." She pulls the spine of the book and in a singular motion the entire wall swings back, and to the left to reveal a stone passageway instantly lit by electric candles. They illuminate a long tunnel that winds into the darkness.

"What I didn't mention is that the previous owner of this house was a paranoid schizophrenic. He was convinced that any success he built would be snatched away by his ex-wife's lawyers. He built this secret passageway so that he could instantly escape should they come calling. This tunnel," she says, peering cautiously inside it, "leads to the very end of the grounds. I have always been too wary to venture inside it. Walter ensures me that it serves its purpose, but even he has not been through to the other end of it."

"Why not?"

"Let me show you something else."

She leads me to a large and ornate living room, which looks out onto the dark expanse of the garden. I notice that this evening the night seems to possess a new depth, as if it were some ever expanding hallway lined with pockets of stars that imbue it with a captivating glow. I see what Georgina means about the evening's mercurial quality, as there is something about this summer night that seems to draw me into it.

Large satin curtains, partially pulled back to reveal the darkness outside, reach from the wall to the ceiling. Francoise moves to the far end of the room, and pulls the right hand curtain back to reveal a small wooden door behind it. Finding my hand with hers, she directs me through. She draws out a small silver key from the end of her necklace and eases it into the lock. The door reveals a small, candlelit chamber, and as we step inside I see a mahogany desk pressed against an Edwardian window. The window is situated precisely in front of the fountains she mentioned, each barely visible in the darkness. The dark red walls are busy with shadows thrown from the smouldering flames in the fireplace. The desk is stacked high with sheaves of white paper, but most of the room is filled with a satin four-poster bed.

"This is where I write," she says, moving to a silver tray on her desk and offering me one of the champagne glasses from it. I wonder if she always has them prepared, or merely saved for certain occasions. "This is my sanctuary, the only place in which I can feel truly secluded. Not even

Walter has access to this room. I keep this place as my inner sanctum."

She sits on the end of the bed, and cautiously I do the same. I study her in the half light; she looks at once determined and yet composed. The darkness outside seems to have crept into the room, and as we sit down I struggle to make out shapes in the dark outside. "You are looking for the fountains?"

A little dizzy, I look out of the window. I can see them now. There are three of them, each spurting silver flumes of water into the sky, to fall into ornate dishes beneath them. "One representing the past, one for the present, and one for the future," she says.

Her voice has a strange effect on me. I look back at her, trying hard to think of something to say. But as I glance at her lips I feel intoxicated, inexplicably bound to her. Even those faint lines on her face fail to detract from the feeling of being overwhelmed by her attention. In the semi-darkness she looks so graceful, so intriguing, that my eyes stayed fixed upon her as she speaks.

A little too quickly, I turn to look at the fountains. "That one is for the future," she says, pointing at the one furthest away, her lips almost on my shoulder now.

The two fountains nearest us are spurting water vigorously into the sky, evoking a feeling of abandon and release. But the one she points out expels water in weak, saccadic bursts, pathetic in comparison to the other two which proudly draw the eye. I look at her face, her lips now so close to mine. I can't think of a response.

"The owner made it so that it was the most powerful of

the three. But for some reason it never was. Still, they are beautiful, aren't they?" she says, looking down at my mouth. The tension between us coils tightly, the pressure rising in my chest, my body fluttering into the rhythm of her breathing. Her lips part, and I wonder if she is going to kiss me as she moves closer still. But suddenly the third fountain bursts into life, greeted by cheers from the guests outside, and I laugh as we part.

As she fills my glass the sweet, heady scent of champagne fills my nostrils. The foam bubbles up in the glass, spilling a little onto our laps. Francoise's movements seem less precise than usual as she smiles, drawing the small bubbles away with a careless hand. "Tell me Vincent. What do you think of The Intimates?" She purses her lips in expectation, her eyes widening as she awaits my answer.

"The people or the book?"

"But they are one and the same."

"Then it is a loaded question."

"All questions are loaded Vincent."

I laugh.

"Do you not agree?"

I peer out into the darkness. "I suppose so. I think that our beloved Intimates are a group of damaged people, perhaps more damaged than we like to admit. We think that because we have certain talents they carry us through life, but in fact each of us has carried themselves through a debilitating void for many years."

"I agree," she says, sipping from her glass.

"I also think that you are a more subtle person than

you pretend to be. And though it is understandable for you to want to organise a party to celebrate your book, I am surprised that you asked us to do so in such a secluded place, where each of our little peculiarities were bound to ferment. I don't believe for one minute that you are unaware of the effect this isolation will have upon your guests. Or that you are unaware of how your reading will have confronted each of us with caricatures of our former selves. So I can only conclude that your speech was keen to disguise the real reason you called this party." As soon as the words have left my mouth I realise they came without pause for thought.

"Which was?"

"To confront each of us with our failure."

She pauses, and peers out at the darkness. "You're right. But it is my failure too. I feel a strong, almost primal urge to confront the seven of us with what we have become. I know that I have softened the blow to myself by bringing it to light on the evening that I'm celebrating my first success. But none of us scrutinise ourselves in the brutal light that we cast upon others.

"I feel we have let ourselves down as a group Vincent. I'm not talking so much of you; you still have time to make your mark. But the others, they all affect me very much. James has become a haunted creature, so delusional that it is becoming quite frightening. And Barbara and Franz console themselves with fading achievements, as if they will somehow excuse their current predicament. It is undignified. I feel compelled to make them address the fact that that they cannot hide from the truth.

"Each of us have let our time pass, not covered ourselves in glory as we were destined too. When obstacles came our way we allowed them to floor us, and we made elaborate excuses to explain why we have remained on the floor. Franz was our pioneer, the man who first awoke us to our gifts, and now he is the most wretched of all of us. No-one has fallen as far as him; it is as if he is a different person. He's falling for Barbara, who ten years ago he would have thought beneath contempt. Now she represents to him some ill-defined world of glamour that he feels he can retract into, like some clammy embryo. And I am no better. One book in a lifetime is not enough to allow me to live with myself, not with the life of opportunity I have been handed.

"I organised tonight, here, to force each of us to cast off these shrouds in whatever manner they've been presented. Whether they came from us, our parents, or this reputedly cursed house. But most of all I did this to address myself."

"Things can change for you now. You are on your way."

"Yes, I suppose." She laughs gaily, pushing her hand through her dark hair before fixing her eyes on me again. "But you know as well as I Vincent, that fire doesn't burn as brightly if you already live in the arms of comfort. We become embodied by a peculiarly unacknowledged shame, which it seems almost ungrateful to admit."

"I know what you mean."

"I know you do. And that is why I wanted to speak with you this evening. As you know, I have always been a huge admirer of your father's work."

"Everyone knows that Francoise. Graham says it's the

reason you were so keen to join our group in the first place."

"He does have a tendency to be rather sharp with his observations. I didn't know who your father was until we became close Vincent, and when I did find out it was merely a pleasant coincidence."

"But you were obsessed with his plays even before they were published, weren't you?"

"Obsessed is a needlessly potent word. I was enchanted by them, that is true. But as you know, ever since we met I've believed that you inherited his talent. I became aware of this when I read the first manuscript you passed amongst us at university. I was saddened to hear that you are now so embarrassed of it. I read it again just before the release of *The Intimates*, and I strongly felt that it is more polished, more ready for consumption than you realise. It is the vehicle by which you can make your own tracks in the world Vincent. I showed it to my agent, and she felt that it could be worth serious consideration."

"Did you tell her who my father was?"

"It doesn't matter Vincent. It really doesn't. What matters is that you shake off this shroud that you have become so accustomed to. You must not be preoccupied with how your work compares with his; you must pursue your own path. I want you to finish your manuscript and let me pass it onto my agent. Because I know that unless you live up to this gift of yours, this peculiar sadness will become a home to you."

A little annoyed, I pass my gaze into the garden. The third fountain is still teeming with strength, flinging water into the sky triumphantly.

"Is it true that he might be joining us tonight? Because if it is, I don't know why you'd let that happen. You know what that would do to this evening for me, and for Barbara. Barbara will kill him."

"Barbara couldn't kill anyone. He is in the country, yes, and he did intimate that he might be in the area tonight."

"Don't let him come here Francoise. You can't."

She smiles in a placatory manner, making it clear that nothing I say will influence her. I realise I cannot even guess what Francoise has in mind for us tonight, let alone alter it.

"Promise me you won't let him come tonight."

"I'll see what I can do. But what do you think about my proposal?"

I think that she is only interested in basking in the light of my father's legacy. I think she wants to be a footnote in his story. I think she wants to feel closer to his talent, and feels she can only do so through his son's highly dubious ability. I think it is vanity that has preceded this offer, that it's the desperation of a generation starting to fade which compels her to revive herself with young blood. I feel angry that she has stated so explicitly what I have long suspected, but this feeling is too raw to be shaped into something constructive now, even if there might be some truth in what she says.

"Perhaps," I answer. "Let me look over it again, and we will see if it lives up to expectation."

She smiles, and I wonder why I haven't realised before that her slender, long hand is resting on the top of my thigh. Francoise has a certain way of speaking; a husky, tender manner in which the most terrible admissions seem tasteful and wrapped in well-meaning. She can make suggestions that are frightening, even dangerous, sound reasonable.

"Don't wait until you have written something which you believe can stand alongside his work. That concern has delayed you enough already," she whispers, drawing a little closer with each word. I can now smell the fragrance of her body, emanating from the pale skin above her cleavage. She strokes the top of my thigh with one trailing finger. Confused by my impulse I look into her face. Her features are as immaculate as ever – wide, Gallic eyes, strangely black in the dark, full lips reaching from the aristocratic structure of her face. Her lips part. The smell of her perfume, mixed with the headiness of the drink makes me draw a little closer to her. "Let me accommodate this frustration of yours," she whispers. "I can make your life… absolutely wonderful Vincent. You know that I can. You have known that for a long time."

She places her hand on the side of my face, and her fingers trail down until one touches my lips. She draws nearer to me, and places my hand on the strap of her dress, which is ready to fall to her elbow with the slightest touch. Her hands motion over mine, making my fingers fall through the strap, and as she eases my hand the strap falls from her dress, revealing the round shape of her breasts, almost exposed under the fallen fabric of her evening gown. "You must let me Vincent."

She moves a polished hand to the other strap of her gown, and shakes her long, glossy hair as she releases it from the slim curve of her shoulder. The dress for a second catches the light from the fire, the side of her body slightly illuminated by the orange and gold flames that capture the canvas of her skin as the dress falls from her shoulders. She moves my hand onto her breast.

"Vincent, we have known each other for a long time. We are The Intimates, that is what they all call us. What happens between us happens between us, and no-one ever needs to know about it. You know that, don't you?"

Her body is immaculate and elegant. The long curve of her torso is slim and pale, and as she parts her thighs the fabric of her dress pulls tight. Her face moves closer to mine, her lips an inch from my ear as she moves my hand down her breasts, to her navel. I feel her breath, hot and perfumed in my ear. "Lie down on the bed Vincent." Her lips close against my cheek, kissing me slowly and softly.

I feel myself being pushed onto the sheets, and she smiles as if encouraged. I'm aware that I must stop this happening, but even as she wraps my bow tie around her fingers, slipping a hand between the buttons of my shirt, I feel convinced that there is no way out, that Francoise has made me want something that I will not be able to refuse. I am pinned like a butterfly, and I know that whatever I say Francoise now has a plan that will not be derailed.

And then I think of Elise.

"I can't," I whisper, as her lips close on my other cheek. I move back. "I mean it, I can't. Don't make me Francoise. Elise is upstairs, and I can't just go back to her if something has happened between us."

She smiles tightly, her eyes carefully considering my profile.

"Francoise, I am sorry, believe me, but I can't. This isn't right. I must think of Elise."

"Ah yes, Elise," she says, her eyes now flashing a little in the dark. "Your little souvenir from your new life. Because that is what she is Vincent, you do know that don't you? You are using her to try and start again, and you're kidding yourself that you can, that you should. Look at the way you've continually evaded her this evening, so that you're never by her side for more than a minute. And look at the way she clings to you – she's so aware that you represent her only chance to escape the mundane. The longer you stay with her the more she'll understand that, and the harder she'll cling. She's terrified that you might shake her off and embrace your true potential. The two of you aren't exactly the portrait of a happy couple. Because you are one of us Vincent. Your desires can only be expressed within us. Anything else will just delay your destiny. I think you're quite aware that you're playing a little game with her."

"And you are playing a little game with me." I sit up, take my tie from her resting fingers and start to wind it back around my neck.

"Don't think that you can continue this sordid new life of yours as if you never met any of us."

"I'm not Francoise. I'm sure I care more about our group than about anything else. But it doesn't mean I have to do things that I am not comfortable with."

For a moment she looks hurt, but then her expression assumes some warmth. "It is the evening Vincent, it has affected me. I'm sorry."

She is trying to get closer to my father through me, and the thought disgusts me. Suddenly I want to be out of the room faster than I possibly can.

"Please," I say. "Take me back to the party."

Enraged, I compose myself, step through the small door and back to the drawing room. I go over to the French windows and pull back the curtain. I can just about make out through the dark that the guests have congregated around the fountain. I think I see Elise look back through the window as Francoise moves behind me. I unlock the door and step outside, Francoise moving slowly in my wake.

A firework fizzes into the air and blooms into an orange bulb, accompanied by a high whoop. As it illuminates I see the bodies, prostrate and skewed, some dancing with their hands in the air around the fountain to rising music.

"Walter, light the lamps," Francoise says, as another firework bursts into life above us. As it lights the side of Francoise's face, she looks changed, suddenly sharper than before. We join the group, the ring of lamps arranged around the fountain containing us in a tight circle.

"Did you show him what you intended to?" Elise asks Francoise. Francoise nods and looks over at the water.

I put my arm around Elise's shoulder. "It's really quite a strange house," I whisper.

"She showed me some of it," Elise says. "Though I got the feeling she kept some of it back from me as well."

"This must be quite an experience for you," Francoise says to her, placing her glass on a nearby table with a snap.

"Is it strange to finally put faces to all of these important names in his life?"

"It's long overdue," Elise answers.

"It would be quite understandable for you to wonder if Vincent had a reason for introducing you to all of us tonight, don't you think?"

"Francoise… "

"Oh Vincent there's nothing you need to hide from her. Elise and I were talking earlier. She was wondering if you'd planned for tonight to be a rather special occasion for the two of you. It's reasonable of her to wonder, isn't it?"

"What's this?" Graham asks, moving over.

"I'm just saying," Francoise repeats, "that Elise would be within her rights to wonder if Vincent has some sort of proposal to make to her this evening."

I can barely make out Elise's expression in the dark, but it seems one of barely concealed fury.

"That's between Vincent and Elise I think Francoise," Graham says. Another firework streaks into the sky, and as it highlights Francoise's face she seems almost drunk on something; so focused that she can barely look straight at Elise.

"Is it really true that Vincent's father is coming tonight?" James asks. "Tell us that isn't the case Francoise."

"It's just a joke," Georgina says, pouring herself champagne and looking inquisitively at Francoise, who in turn looks up at the dying embers of the firework. "It *is* just a joke, isn't it Francoise?"

"Tonight is an opportunity to bring people together, those for whom a reunion is long overdue. This night is bigger than I am, so none of you must hold me to account for its actions."

"What you are trying to say then, is that you have invited Vincent's father and that he is on his way. Is that right?" Graham asks.

"Francoise, you wouldn't do that to me. It would destroy our evening," I say.

"It wouldn't be so bad, would it?" Elise asks, and James and Graham shoot her a look. Barbara is dancing on the edge of the fountain with Franz, looking for her lost high heel.

"Francoise," James hisses. "If he comes here tonight Barbara will kill him. No arguments, no uncomfortable silences. Barbara will simply kill him."

Francoise smiles wanly, and continues to dance to music that seems only audible to her.

"Did you hear what he said Francoise?" Graham asks. "Or are you still pretending to be decadent?"

"No-one is going to get killed," Francoise says. "All of us are such *good friends*. All of us are so *Intimate*." She says the word as if it is now a curse, and then she starts to dance towards the fountain, leaving the rest of us to desperately read each other's expressions.

"I hope she is going to warn Barbara," James says. "I am not looking forward to at least one of us being reduced to rubble by that man."

Graham puts his hand on my shoulder. "If he comes, we keep him at arm's length. He is just one man, and his opinions are just that. We all seem to think that because he's quite successful his views are somehow gospel. They're not. He's an unhappy fellow, who uses other people as punch bags on a regular basis. But this is a party, and we won't let him, or her," he says, looking over at Francoise, "ruin it."

"Why does Barbara hate your father so much?" Elise asks me.

"Soon after they fell out, on that ridiculous childhood holiday," Graham says, "Sean appeared on a primetime television chat show. The show featured another actor who had just starred in a film with Barbara, her last major film as it happened. Barbara's name was mentioned by the host and Sean just took her... to pieces. He was truculent even at the start of the interview, when he talked about how difficult it must be for her to act behind a plastic mask. At first the audience were tittering along. But when he called her a 'wilting plastic flower' the audience stopped laughing. 'But you and Barbara go back a long way,' the host said. 'Surely you are just teasing her.' 'No I'm not,' Sean replied. 'Every day the film industry corrodes a little more because of talentless, vapid people like her who fill our screens with artless performances.' That's right, isn't it?" he says, looking over at me. I nod.

"'At the very least,' he continues, his gruff voice mimicking my father's, 'there should be a union to stop women like her ever appearing on celluloid. At the most I would propose specimens like her are lined up against a wall and shot, to prevent them ever touting their withered wares on the world stage again.'"

Elise exhales in shock. "I am surprised you don't know the story," James says. "You must watch television rather sparingly."

"It was a few years ago," I offer. "Few people even know who Barbara was."

"Still, it was a vicious and cruel thing to say, and I think it would be best if Barbara was not informed he might be coming tonight."

As if on cue, a wail goes up from the fountain, and Barbara throws her cocktail glass towards Francoise.

"Has Francoise lost all semblance of tact in the last few minutes?" Graham asks. Through the half-light I see Barbara throwing her arms up, clasping them to her face and then flying into Franz's arms for comfort; a ridiculously emotive gesture.

Francoise steps back from them, takes a sip of wine, and then makes her way over to us.

"Bearing her response in mind, do you think it might be a good idea to call Sean and ask him to postpone his visit?" James asks her.

"Barbara's had too much to drink, that's all," Francoise says, picking at her dress.

"Francoise, what the hell is going on?" James says, his voice rising. "I can't think why on earth you would do this to our little group, to Vincent at the very least. Call ahead, get him to cancel. What is in this for you?"

"There's nothing in this for me."

"Are you after material for your second book or something? *The Demise of The Intimates*?"

"He probably won't come anyway," Francoise whispers.

"There really is no need for everyone to get so het up."

"You're up to something Francoise," I start, as Elise takes my arm. "You're playing some sort of game with us, and I'm pretty surprised by it."

The same bemused smile stays on her lips, and then she looks back at me as if suddenly concerned. "Vincent, allow me to speak with you for a moment. People, please excuse us."

She draws me quickly towards the house. I hear Elise, James and Graham confer in mystified tones as Francoise leads me towards the French windows and into the kitchen.

"I'm not leaving Elise for long," I say, as she brushes aside a butler, who's slicing peppermint leaves on the kitchen table.

"We'll take over for a minute Oscar, thank you," she says, scooping ice from a silver vat and frittering it into large cocktail glasses. "Close the door on the way out."

She looks quickly at me. She seems a little unhinged now, drunk perhaps – and yet somehow more determined than ever. "If you are angry with me Vincent, it is because you don't understand me. Of course I don't want to cause conflict between anyone. Tonight is an opportunity to build bridges between people who are treating one another in a way they should not."

"That does not apply to Barbara and my father. Their disagreement goes far beyond that."

"I'm afraid that my intentions behind this evening apply to them too." She pours vodka into each glass, the slightly blue liquid running between her long fingers as she transfers it quickly. "It applies to you and your father, and it applies to the two of them. Vincent, Barbara and your father go back a very long way. I feel that tonight your father is ready to apologise to her, to make amends. You see, she does not hate him merely because of this silly little holiday and this barbed little chat show appearance. There's something you must know, Vincent, and perhaps tonight is not the best time to tell you this, but I must have you on my side if this is going to work." She sets down the scoop and leans against the counter, considering me carefully before she speaks.

"It's your father, Vincent, that got Barbara pregnant with Georgina and her brother many years ago, and who in so doing ruined Barbara's career."

I shake my head; wondering if I have heard correctly.

"You deserve to know the truth. If neither of them have the gall to tell you then someone should, though it is ultimately your decision what you do with the information. Barbara and your father had a brief affair when she acted in his first play, and she fell pregnant soon after with twins.

"Many years later, on this infamous holiday, Barbara confronted him and told him that Georgina had a right to know who her father was, that you had a right to know she was your half-sister. Your father was ashamed that he had cheated on your mother during their courtship, and insisted he would never do anything to besmirch her reputation – though of course he was not to know that she would soon pass away. He threatened to ruin Barbara's career if she ever breathed a word of their liaison to anyone. Around the time of the chat show he briefly had reason to believe that she might do that, and so he destroyed her publicly as a little warning as to what he was capable of. Since then, of course, Barbara has kept her counsel. Though the rest of the world knew that her time had passed, Barbara always held onto the belief that a resurgence of fame was imminent. She kept her secret safe, so that your father could do her reputation no more harm."

"Georgina – is my half-sister? But how do you know this?"

"You know I am a devoted follower of your father Vincent, and if it is not too presumptuous of me I like to think that over the years we have become friends. At times he has seen me as a confidante, even if sometimes I have had to read a little between the lines of what he says."

"You mean that you don't even know if this is true?"

"It is true Vincent," she says, dismissively. "And tonight I have asked your father to come because I feel he is now ready to make amends with Barbara."

"Well judging by her performance out by the fountain, I don't think Barbara *is* ready to make amends. Even if what you say is true, tonight still does not seem a good night for anything that delicate to come out into the open."

"Tonight is the perfect night for this Vincent, don't you see? Tonight is about facing our pasts, taking on our future with veracity. Tonight is about confronting our truths Vincent."

"Well why don't we start to confront your truths a little more then Francoise? How about it? The real reason you are trying to mend all of my father's relationships, yes?

Because I think it all comes down to a very simple desire to have a role in his life. It's nothing to do with wanting what's best for us; it's a way for you to handle this obsession you have for him, which you have had since long before we met. Am I right?"

"You're just being childish now Vincent."

"No, I'm not. I don't even know if I can handle this information tonight, but Georgina most certainly cannot. She and her mother are very close to ending their temperamental relationship once and for all, and I won't be the one to tell her this news this evening. You should wait until this can be dealt with sensitively Francoise, and judging by the way you are teasing Elise I would say that is beyond your capacity right now."

"I was just having a little fun with Elise," she says, as she pours bright green liquid into the cocktail glasses, scattering over them the shredded leaves and then stirring each with a long mixer.

"That is it Francoise. I have looked to you for guidance for much of my life, but tonight you are treating people like toys, and their pasts like scenery that you can reshuffle at will. And you cannot do that. I don't know what has happened to you, but tonight you have lost something, something that always prevented you from being this person."

"If you are angry towards me because I teased Elise then I am sorry." She sips a cocktail, and blinks slowly in pleasure. "Wonderful," she says. "I was a little mean to her, but I will make it up to her now Vincent. Now take a cocktail."

Francoise draws me outside into the still night, her guests looking expectantly up at her. She hands a slightly bewildered Elise one of the potent-looking cocktails. "I don't think that I've shown you the jewellery left to me with this house, have I Elise? I think I'm a little old to pull some of it off, but some of the pieces might suit a woman with your style. Would you be interested in having a look at them?"

Elise looks up, relieved and perhaps excited, and excuses me with a wave as the two of them sweep into the house.

As they walk away Georgina and Graham look over, but I am still too angry with Francoise to meet their eye. Perhaps I am slightly frightened too, frightened of how I will feel when I look up and see Georgina in a new light. Already I am aware that what Francoise has said rings true. I realise that it makes sense; it explains how the bond between Georgina and I always surpassed the mere proximity of youth. I understand now the protective, slightly aloof manner with which we have long dealt with one another. Perhaps somehow we both knew all along. It would explain the way that, for some unknown reason, we were always unable to see one another in a romantic light – however politically helpful it sometimes might have been to do so.

I don't look up, but can sense already that Georgina is lingering by Graham's side, curiously looking over at me. Without even meeting her eye I feel then as if another shard of my fragmented, secretive inner life now fits with the world. I wonder if Georgina already knows, and if she does not then whether she is easily reading my body language right now. I wonder if with every second that she looks over she is learning what I have just been told, and that thought starts to unnerve me.

From the fountains I can just about make out a light in the poolroom, and as I move nearer I see a shadow sweep across the interior. It is vague and dispersed, but distinct enough to grasp my attention. As the others turn into one another, as if consoling, I move over towards it. I can see the neon blue of the water in the pool, the submerged lamps throwing the movement from the ripples onto the wall. As I step to the window I see Franz, his head bowed, amongst the cheap furniture that Francoise has installed as a poolside lounge.

As I step inside, a blast of music fills the air. At first it sounds indulgent, but as my ears adjust I realise there is something addictive about it. A worn, hungry voice clamours over the building guitars. Chattering drums rise from the background, eager to step to the fore. Franz is stooped over a record player, adjusting the sound. I hand him a half-empty bottle of wine from a nearby table. He turns to face me, smiling to see that he is not alone. Yet even as he greets me something is retained in his eyes, as though he is still in thrall of the music. His eyes focus on the record player; he takes a gulp of wine before holding my elbow as the music starts to peak.

"Listen – " he says, as if preparing me for something transcendent. The circling riff tightens like a knot in the stomach, creating an almost unbearable tension. The voice rises to achieve the high notes, before finally hinging itself around the hook of the song with a glorious abandon that raises the hairs on my neck. As the cymbals swell the song crashes to a halt. I feel exhilarated and inspired.

He looks up at me and in the garish light for a second he looks ten years younger – his fringe still plastered to the side of his face, the circling lights illuminating him as he carefully manages the glare of the crowd, who respond so urgently to his caresses. His guitar is slim and lethal, its many cuts seem like war wounds from a battle against the mundane. A ravenous roar fills his ears, electrifies him. But as the cymbals fade I see in the half-light that is no longer the case. He is older now; his nicotine-tinged fingers twitch with less precision. His body is less contained, he no longer has that strange sexual energy I remember him using to stalk stages in his youth. He shakes his head, smiling to console himself.

"What do you think?" he asks, nodding me towards the answer he wants.

"It was incredible."

"It still is." He smiles, lopsidedly. His face is flushed with pride; a powerful feeling which I suspect now visits him rarely. I want to ask why he has come here, alone, to listen to his own seven-year-old album. But there's a clammy scent of desperation around him, and I feel inclined to treat him gently, to nourish him somehow. It's a feeling which sits uncomfortably with me, and I resent him for forcing me to play that role.

I am used to Franz circling me, building my confidence with hands that move in waves of encouragement.

I am used to his eyes lighting up as he goads me to reveal some secret promise that I know I have. I am used to him insisting that I am the person I want to be, and not the wretched person I often feel I am. Usually his potent mixture of aftershave and perspiration signifies that inspiration is on its way. It upsets me that he now wants me to somehow build him up. It would be like seeing your father cry – though your reaction is to help, it feels well beyond your capacity, terrifying even.

"Towards the end of that song, there were shivers going down my spine," I continue. He looks up at me, his face wide with unmasked pleasure. He's heard this response many times, but hearing it now clearly relieves him. My approval seems to offer him a surge he will ask of strangers for the rest of his life. He moves over to a lounger, taking a gulp of wine as he settles down.

I feel compelled to snap him out of this reverie. "Do you remember when you taught me how you channel all your negativity into the way you move onstage? Do you remember that?"

He looks at me as if waking from a dream. I press on, eager to make him emerge from this chrysalis as the invigorated man he once was. "It was just after your first gig," I say, walking up and down in front of him as he cradles a wine glass. Something starts to move in his eyes.

"I asked you how you knew exactly what to do with your hands on stage, how to dance to the song, what to say to the audience. You took me backstage and you told me that at any concert a unique motion is lingering in the room, and it is the performer's job – whether a musician, singer or comedian to instantly use it. To use the moments when the crowd offers you wild acclaim to find that motion and tap into it. You told me that to be a performer, in any walk of life, I had to train myself to find that channel instantly and dwell in it for the duration that I am on show."

I am circling him now, wrapping my determination to hoist him from the past around him. He begins to nod, at first weakly, but soon with sharpness – like a battered boxer being coaxed by his coach to face the final rounds.

"And I asked you what you do if you don't sense that motion in the room. If you are met with nothing but apathy or negativity. And you taught me that then, especially then, there was energy to be sourced that's more powerful than any other. You taught me that negativity was an emotion easier to use than any other. That in that circumstance a performer should make themselves a medium for the anger in the room. That the performer is the only one in the room privileged enough to act as a mirror for everything the audience is feeling. You said they can offer the audience a spectacle, a cathartic spectacle for them to vicariously live through for the duration they are on stage. They can turn that negativity and apathy into something beautiful. Do you remember?"

He looks up, smiling as if faintly embarrassed by his previous passion. "I do remember. Did I really say all of that?"

"You did." I am nearly jabbing him with my finger now, as if channelling my own resentment into a need to inspire him. "You said that the most glorious sensation an artist could feel was that all his peculiarities had been validated through his performance, through his art. That every artist strived for a state of complete self-realisation, which drove them to slave away at often ignored works into the dead of the night. You must remember Franz – I have committed your lessons to memory, every one of them."

"All of his peculiarities? Really? But you gain more peculiarities with time Vincent. Did I know that then? The world breaks down your defences, and plays havoc with your beliefs. It's like a bull in the china shop of your mind, leaving you to pick over the fragments it leaves for the rest of your days. The world is so relentlessly accurate with its cruelty."

"But you must learn to use your ability to articulate such concepts into making art again Franz. Be a conduit, as only you can do. You were the one who taught me that it was possible."

"You need confidence to do that Vincent, confidence that you can tap into a vague feeling that's hanging over a room full of strangers. You cannot fake that confidence; it must emanate from you. How can I have that confidence now? The closest I can get to it is through these songs, which I play to remind myself of it. Now Pablo is gone, these songs are all I have left of that time."

It occurs to me that somewhere in his body is a demon, which he longs to reawaken. His face assumes a look of bitter resignation. In his heart he knows that demon has gone to sleep, forever. That he lost contact with it when Pablo, his song-writing partner, died. He knows only too well that his hour has passed, that he will stay now in a state of decline. I sit on the edge of the couch opposite him and sip from my glass.

He looks up at me apologetically. "I know what you mean Vincent; I must try to practice what I once preached. Pablo was the first person to tap into my ability, and I just need to find a way to now access it without him. I'm sure if I *needed* it back I could get it. But I'm not so young anymore."

It intrigues me to hear him talk of his talent as I'd thought of it. As a separate entity that must be found, as a monster that wrecks everything beautifully. Looking at the queasy compromise he has become, it seems now more like a feral animal, which passes between people with no loyalty or concern, leaving tattered lives in its wake. That preys upon the beautiful and the wicked, and commands them to do its work until they become seduced by it, unable to leave it. It defines them, drains them, and then abandons them – leaving broken shells like Franz behind in their wake. To cower in empty rooms at parties, trying to relive it in little snatches. It embodied Franz just for one record, but without Pablo there to nurture it, slipped away as easily as it came. Now it possesses new flesh.

Since then mere blood and muscle have kept Franz alive, but nothing tears at his veins anymore. Franz turns to face me, his eyes widening.

"You weren't there during those glory years Vincent. You don't understand how much they change you. You look at me and you want me to be the man that I once was. But that kind of adulation, that kind of lifestyle, it alters you. It makes you accustomed to getting a huge reaction when you enter a room, living with a state of mind so transcendental it's almost impossible to return to the real world again.

"When I disappeared from your life for those few years, for much of it I was holed up in the Chelsea Hotel. I had three model girlfriends and an acoustic guitar for company, and I thought I could do no wrong by any of them. I felt as if the world had opened up to me like an oyster, as if everything was there for the taking. If I fancied another mans girlfriend, I didn't hesitate. I had an enormous, constant sense of entitlement. Now I see the error of my ways, and yet that feeling was so addictive that to now be merely human just seems... undignified.

"When Pablo and I met in recording studios, every time we picked up our guitars we wrote something special. For those few years we were just in that wonderful zone. With him I had a *need* to impress, to try and better him. Like the feelings you get what you fall in love – you can't recreate them with mere determination. You can't judge me for being unable to bring that back. How do you expect me to have that strength?

"Pablo was my best friend as well as my song-writing partner. He was the man whose talent handed me the treasures of the world. And yet when he was in the grips of heroin addiction I was carrying on with those three models and not responding to his calls. I became so angry that I was no longer the centre of his world, that he cared more for drugs, that I shut him out. By the time his addiction became life-threatening I wouldn't even answer the phone to him. When he finally died, in wretched and desperate circumstances, I was the ninth person to hear of it. With what we had been through I should have been the first – and yet success had changed me so much that I barely felt it when the news came through. That pain is still with me now though, as much as ever. I need fame and money to numb it, to take it away. It is the only way that the world can make sense to me again."

He looks up at me. I see that his eyes are bloodshot and his skin pallid. The movement of his body now lacks the charisma which once seemed to course so naturally through him. It is as if it has been resolutely switched off, by the decided push of a button.

"Is this why you chase after Barbara, Franz? Because you think she offers you a way back into that world?"

"Barbara has it in her to be successful again Vincent. She has that special spark, I see it in her. Barbara understands how the world works, how it closes a door to us and how tenacious we must be to open it again. I know she still has it within her Vincent, and when I spend time with her it comforts me to know that I am not alone. She may not articulate what she and I have in common, but she knows we are two of a kind. I feel so sure that she still has enough vibrancy, enough colour, that the two of us together can find a way back into our pasts."

I want to grab him and shake him. For confusing his unique ability with her self-centredness. For trying to find himself solely through what he once had. For buying into Barbara's dangerous and ill-defined delusions.

"Franz, you must take in what I am saying. You had – have – a gift that is rare and in many ways unprecedented. But the only way you will rediscover it is through clarity and discipline, the two traits you taught me to value above all others. Barbara does not have talent. She will offer you nothing but confusion. You must not allow yourself to be drawn in by her shabby and faded glamour. She is so much *older* than you."

"Don't make the mistake of treating me as you want me to be Vincent. Your father does that with you, and look at the harm it has done. Vincent, if your father comes tonight, stand your ground. Be firm about who you are, and do not allow his loathing to impact upon you."

For the first time I recognise the voice that comforted me for a long time. But then he looks down.

"I look at you, Vincent, and I see disappointment. You want me to pull you from your rut, but you can't expect me to do that anymore. All of my strength is used up by merely keeping *me* alive."

He looks broken, and I wonder if should put my arm around him. But that seems such a reversal of our previous relationship that I decide I shouldn't. Or can't.

"Francoise has advised me to finish my manuscript and submit it to her agent. She thinks it could really take me somewhere. Do you think she might be right?"

He cocks his head to one side; his expression suggests that he is still in thrall of that faded music. "I think the rewards of success are more complicated than someone like her can imagine." His eyes look utterly hollow, like an animal's footprints in snow.

"Lets be brutal for a moment Vincent," he continues. "Francoise has created one work of promise, during her late middle-age. Barbara had a couple of wonderful films and then suffered a crisis of confidence. But my work lives on around the world, in people's hearts and minds. None of The Intimates understand success like I do Vincent. You want realistic advice, talk to me about what I have been through."

"I don't need advice, Franz. I have had enough of that from my father. I want to be *inspired*."

"Then buy yourself a self-help book."

As he busies himself with that CD, still too self-consumed to acknowledge me entirely, I suddenly find him distasteful, repulsive even. He clings to anyone who praises his past achievements, but he has no regard for their concerns. He has the self-absorption of one who's lived his life with a sense of entitlement, who has no gratefulness for the pleasures the world has let him indulge, who doesn't realise the void most people negotiate on a daily basis. His solipsism sickens me, and I feel glad fate has forced him to adjust.

It is his fault if he can't, life does not bend towards our every wish. People tell him he still has the gift, but it's like a wife who reassures a man that she's his only one, when it's obvious her attentions are now elsewhere. He passes through this routine of self-assurance as if forever hoping to rediscover something in its fading circles. He moves in increasingly complex patterns, looking for something to trigger that rush. He can't finish any new pieces because he knows they will pale in comparison to his previous work. It is almost as though he's condemned himself to never feel again.

"We were good, weren't we?" he says, smiling weakly and turning way from me. "We had something really good."

Remorse occupies his face, and then he suddenly looks up brightly. Barbara is hitching up her skirt as she steps towards the fountain outside. As if something blissful has occurred to him, as if all his woes are suddenly gone, he calls out her name. It surprises me how quickly a woman's movement can dispel a man's sadness.

I watch him rush outside to lift the train of her dress. Barbara kicks off her heels, preparing herself for the chill of the water. I walk out behind him, contemplating how happy he now looks despite what he has just told me. Graham joins me at my side, and we watch the two of them. Since I last saw Graham he's wrapped one of Francoise's scarves around his neck and his eyelids are now smeared with glitter. He looks as if he is finally beginning to relax in the company of his friends.

"There's something so messy about Franz's self-pity," he says, exhaling smoke. "And his recent solo work."

I laugh, as if mock-annoyed at this slight. His face breaks open in a knowing laugh. "It's good to see you. Finally, we are given the opportunity to speak."

"I've had some pretty unusual conversations this evening. And it doesn't seem right that a chat with a transvestite will come as light relief."

"Jesus, that does throw your evening into perspective.

How was James this evening? Does he still turn into a bunny-boiler at the mere mention of Carina's name?"

"Very much so, yes," I say with a laugh. "But whenever I try to defend her, a little voice tells me to be very careful not to let on how I feel about her."

"He still has no idea?"

"He doesn't want to have any idea Graham."

"He must be the only one of us still in denial about that situation then. Has Elise picked up on anything?"

"I think she might have done."

"She was bound to sooner or later. How has she handled everything this evening?"

"Like everyone else, she's acted in a manner that I could not possibly have predicted."

"I want to see this mini health spa Francoise has built herself. Shall we?" The two of us trail into the pool room, looking around us to make sure no-one is to disturb our conversation. Puffing his cigarette Graham reaches down to untie his shoes, before rolling up his trousers and dipping his feet into the pool. As he turns round to look at me the streak of glitter on his cheek illuminates. I crouch down next to him, watching the artificial blue of the water move under the dipped lamps on the wall. Franz and Barbara's excited screams are audible behind us.

Perhaps it is my drunkenness, but there seems to be something very beautiful about the plastic sheen of the water, mixed carefully to look natural when inspection reveals it to be anything but. I think of James' enrapture for the books in the library, and the way this turquoise water similarly enchants me. I wonder if people who own houses like this ever consider them from the perspective of others. What may seem shabby and incidental on the surface through fresh eyes can reveal an essence they might otherwise neglect. Catching these half-formed thoughts, Graham meets my eye.

"Francoise wants us all to take a long hard look at ourselves, doesn't she?" he says. "I think that's the intention behind this evening."

"I think so. She's appointed herself as our moral guardian, or something."

"Like a sort of Gallic Jiminy Cricket?"

"Something like that. She means well though. I think."

We fall quiet. I notice that swirling around our pale feet is a spiral of rose petals, caught in a whirlpool made by their motion. We both move our feet in time, our eyes fixed on those dancing red curls. For a while they stay in that slipstream but then spin out of our control, floating back into the body of water.

"The last thing I need is another parent figure," he says. "Trying to make me fit their requirements of how I should be. My father is 70, but he's still struggling with the idea of a son who's a surgeon but also a transvestite." He laughs and looks over my shoulder at the fountain. Glancing at his profile his seeming contradictions make perfect sense to me. There's the tightness in his jaw line and the high set eyes which are precise and surgical. Yet the makeup under his eyes and the ruffle of his scarf fit with the effeminacy an altruistic role sometimes implies.

"Do you also see yourself as a transvestite now then?"

He considers the question with a look that's very

childlike, given what has been asked.

"I think I always have been Vincent. I think it's just that I've become more confident about it. Some of my happiest memories are of being temporarily left alone at home by my parents. Within seconds I'd be at my mother's dresser, clumping about in oversized heels with ridiculous clouds of rouge on my cheeks. I must have looked like a Victorian toy soldier. Had my father returned home at that moment, I would have been beaten to within an inch of my life.

"I remember the ecstasy of first going to a nightclub wearing eyeliner. Drenched in hairspray and glitter, dancing to Lou Reed records. I felt as if I was living on the outside, in a realm that most people could never enter. For so long I had felt completely alone, but makeup made my isolation feel special. The world came to life – the streets were no longer grey and cold, they sparkled with sordid possibility. But the most resonant pleasures in our lives are always individually defined. When you expect the world to appreciate them they simply expose their own bland uniformity. I learnt that the more unusual you are, the more personalised pleasures the world reveals to you."

"I remember when we used to climb trees in the summer holidays," I say. "You were the biggest risk taker of all. But when the evening came you'd always start suggesting that we play fancy dress. That would be the point at which I'd start to think about going home."

"Poor you," he laughs. "Having a perfectly innocent day, and then having me suggest something truly subversive at the end of it. I wasn't the only daredevil amongst us though, was I? Do you remember the time you climbed the one tree in your garden that your father had forbidden us to go near?"

The memory of that afternoon, still painful, flashes before my eyes. Perhaps reacting to my expression, Graham lowers his voice. "It was his favourite tree, the great sycamore at the foot of the garden, the one he watched from his top floor study when he was writing. And he said that it was the only tree that you shouldn't climb, and that if you did you would be very sorry. So you did what any schoolboy would have done under the circumstances."

"I still feel guilty about that Graham," I laugh. "I'm so sorry. I thought he was out. I wanted so badly to get back at him for ignoring me. But I was cowardly, so I got back at him in a way that I hoped he would never know. By climbing that stupid, sacred tree of his. But I soon learnt that he wasn't out at all – he'd just left his study for a few moments. He came back to see this muddy kid clambering up his beloved tree at the foot of the garden.

I remember the roar that he gave out; it reverberated around the garden. I instantly opened my arms and fell about ten feet, grabbed onto one of the lower branches. 'Get down!' you screamed. 'He's going to kill us!' I was so much more scared of him than of the fall. When I got to the ground my arms were bruised, my knees were cut and bloody and you said – "

"That I'd never seen you look that frightened before. And then he loomed over and grabbed you by the arm, and I was so terrified of what he might do Vincent, his rage was so terrifying that I reacted – "

"You told him that it was you who'd climbed the tree.

I'll never forget that. And he looked at me and said, 'Is this true? Because if not you have just doubled your punishment.' And you insisted." The memories are raw and clear now, if a little disordered. "'It was me,' you said. 'Vincent told me not to do it but I ignored him.' And then that moment of mute rage when he looked between the two of us, and it occurred to me – "

"That he'd hoped it was you in the tree?"

"Yes," I answer. "I think you're right. But then his rage was so enormous, so overwhelming, that he couldn't stop himself. There in front of me, he beat you. He even dropped your shorts to do it, didn't he?"

"You kept opening your mouth, to say it was you. That he shouldn't beat me, but my eyes were begging you not to as I knew it would just mean both of us getting punished."

"That was my punishment. He knew it. To let you take the blame for me, he knew that would destroy me. And it did. You were such a good friend Graham. You really didn't need to do that for me."

"I don't know why I did!" he laughs. "But I remember afterwards, looking at him and thinking how incredibly *unfair* it was. I had no idea life could be so wrong. And him, shamefaced, saying to me, 'It's for your own good Graham. Your father would have done the same had he been here.' It was pathetic. He seemed to want me to thank him for his brutality, to look up at him through the tears and congratulate him for being such a man. And of course I didn't; I kept completely silent. And I felt that in some little way I got level with him at that moment. By seeing how embarrassed he was with his own rage."

He kicks at the water. "My father would have beaten me too, but not as savagely. He knew about my little secrets, he just needed to catch me in the act. Our fathers were similar in that way, both of them made us hide a great deal. That sense of having a certain state of mind that you sometimes must express – it's enough to define you. I think if I'd not have had a father who found such activities repulsive, I would probably not have gained as much pleasure from them, funnily enough."

"If he can't take in your contradictions, I reckon he hasn't spent enough time with you while being openminded," I suggest.

He smiles. "I know what you mean. Through my eyes, I make perfect sense. My maternal instincts are put into my work, which is a perfect continuation of my lifestyle. But to him it's a maddening contradiction. He's pleased that his son has an enviable career, but infuriated that the honour that brings him is tempered by me queening it about in drag. But what do I do? Work four days a week at the hospital and spend the rest of my time wearing a suit from Next?"

"No. I can't see you in anything off the rack."

"Just one reason he'll never be happy," he laughs. He exhales, smoke passing from his mouth into a cloud above us. "People don't see. They spend their lives in compromised and unhappy states because they don't stumble across a state of mind in which they feel liberated. I'm straight, but I probably never feel more like myself than when I'm wearing a dress. In a way, I feel fortunate. At least I have found a state of mind which I can call home.

But the world, perhaps through envy or fear, forces me to hide it away.

"It holds me back professionally Vincent, of course it does. How can I push for consultancy posts when my cross-dressing is bound to be brought up by the review panel? We supposedly live in enlightened times, but my rivals have my head in a noose if they find out about my nightlife. The insinuation behind Francoise calling this party is that we should take a long hard look ourselves, and get over whatever restricts us. But she doesn't see that I have already done that. I'm not like Franz or Barbara, hankering after adolescent glory. I'm more successful than ever, approaching the top of my game. Unlike them, I do not hold *myself* back. It is the rest of the world that restrains me."

"What Francoise has shown me this evening is that you shouldn't compromise. If other people can't get their head around you, forget them. Concern yourself with embodying your own contradictions as fully as you can. If you are open about your own individuality then your rivals will have no hold over you. Now I'm not saying you should go into the surgery theatre in full drag Graham, I'm not saying that." He smiles. "But I am saying that you should try to be as open about your life as you reasonably can. If you do, you'll find that people quickly fall into two camps – those you want to know, and those you don't."

He considers this for a second. Then we both look at each other and laugh at our sudden seriousness. Whenever we're in each other's company we seem to use the time to steady ourselves against the world.

"Unfortunately, one of the people who'll fall into the latter camp is my father," he says.

"But how often does anybody accept all our contradictions? Barely ever. They all try and mould us in some way. Your father probably *won't* appreciate all the self-actualisation you've achieved. What Francoise says stings me, because I haven't achieved my potential. I'd nearly convinced myself that I didn't have it in me, so that was alright. But she's reminded me that weight is still there, because I *have* got something."

"I think you have too," Graham replies. "I think you've tried hard to justify your situation, when the answer has been in front of you all along. You want to write, but your father's judgements have stopped you. You need to face up to him. Everyone is so frightened of him coming here this evening, of being badly wounded by one of his off-the-cuff remarks. But I know that if you're bold you can face up to him."

His conviction unnerves me, though I suspect he might be right.

"He has a torrent inside him Graham. I don't know if I can face it this evening."

"You can Vincent. You can because you must. Do you remember when we used to jump from the pier into the sea at low tide, just for the rush? Do you remember that your father specifically told us not to, that one day we'd hurt ourselves? It was me who encouraged us to keep doing it, and so it was fitting that one day I gashed my leg open doing it. And your father saw the blood and his face went – but before he could open his mouth you said, 'Did you forget the first aid kit Dad? I told you Graham was going to hurt himself riding his bike one day, and you still forgot it, didn't you?' That look of rage disappeared from his face because you'd shocked him; you had him on the back foot.

"If you confront him, he will be so surprised that he will probably just take it. Look at how trapped each of us are – in our little delusions, our little predicaments. If just one of us faces up to our situation it will offer all of us a way out."

"But how can I just confront him? If he's to be convinced, he'll need to know what my plan is, and I don't have one. What am I going to tell him, that I'm going to find a quiet desk in a corner somewhere and write something as universally appealing as his first two plays? I don't even have a plan!"

"He doesn't know that. And he doesn't need to know details. He just needs to be surprised by your boldness."

He finishes his cigarette, and we spend a little more time watching those swirling petals beneath us. Some have escaped that motion we cast upon them and fluttered to the surface, now bobbing on the little waves we've made.

"This conversation is *so* male."

"However much makeup you wear, you don't stop being an archetypal man," I reply.

"What a horrible fate," he says, throwing the remainder of his cigarette into the water. "Come on. There's something inside that I want to show you, that I think might be of interest."

I follow him back through the patio and into the drawing room. "This way," he says, walking up a long and ornate staircase. As we reach the top of the stairs he loses himself for a second, and then points down the hallway. "It's along here," he whispers. Gold lights hung in small stone baskets line the passageway, dimly lighting the path to Francoise's room. As we move down I see that on either side of the hallway there's a series of alcoves, gold strip lamps lighting up the paintings embedded within them. In each one, satin curtains are parted to reveal the picture, but as we reach the end of the hallway one painting's curtains are closed, hiding it from passing observers.

"Have a look at this." After looking each way to check that Francoise is not nearby, Graham parts the curtains to reveal the picture.

Immediately I am startled by the portrait. Unlike the tasteful, sparse paintings around it, this one is vivid and confrontational.

It depicts a slender, waif-like man who is facing the viewer. His skin has a faint grey hue and he is clasping the chair he is sat upon on, which is on the flat roof of a house. Behind him are the vibrant colours of a setting sun. The streaks of scarlet and burgundy in the sky suggest a Mediterranean climate, though his distressed confinement to the chair denies him the spectacle of it. Standing over him is a Greek-looking woman in a domestic dress, her hair scraped back into a bun. Her features are attractive, but the expression she gives the man is one of amused scorn. In one hand she holds a large pair of scissors, and as I look closer I see that half the man's hair is lying around him, having been cut or torn from his head. The woman is leaning in and opening the scissors as if to remove the rest of it. I see how terrified the man is. He looks utterly emasculated, and he clasps the chair that imprisons him as if his life depends on it. There is a gold plate at the side of the picture. *A Biblical Scene* it says. 'By James Hewston'.

"This is one of James' paintings?" I ask.

"It's one of his post-accident pieces."

"I had no idea they were like this."

"Disturbing, isn't it?" he says, craning into it and then stiffening up.

"It seems to depict a morbid terror of the power women have over him. As if they are all evil and oppressive, as well as potential castrators. It is a biblical scene; one of Samson in distress. He lost all his powers once Delilah had his hair removed. And do you remember what happened next?"

I look back at the picture, casting my mind back to school. "After Delilah had his hair cut, even God deserted him and he was captured by Philistines who... "

"Who put his eyes out. Samson's downfall came because of misplaced trust in a woman. This is James' self-portrait, Vincent, don't you see? He blames Carina for the loss of his vision, for the loss of his gift. Look closer. Does the woman in the picture remind you of any-one?"

I lean in, wary of what I will see. But from the high cheekbones, and the rich dark eyes it is evident that the woman in the painting strongly resembles Carina.

"How come no-one's said anything before? And how

come Francoise has this painting in her house, hidden away?"

"No-one has said anything because everyone is scared of him. Everyone is frightened of how he will react when confronted with his take on the past." I consider whether I should tell Graham about my conversation with James earlier, but decide not to.

"Francoise bought this painting out of pity," he continues. "James' inability to distinguish colour explains why the picture is so garish, why none of them sell anymore. But the real reason Francoise closed the veil over this painting is because she doesn't want Carina to see it tonight."

"I don't blame her," I answer. "Carina would be extremely hurt to learn that he blames her for his downfall."

"That's right. And that's why I wanted to show you this. I am worried about James, Vincent. He hasn't just lost his ability." Graham starts to look serious, lowering his voice and looking around him. "He is also starting to lose his mind. Since the accident he has developed a hatred of women that is becoming very dangerous."

"He believes they've stripped him of his potency, doesn't he?"

"Yes. He thinks they're all sadists, who set traps for him and laugh when he's ensnared. Did you hear about the Belgian waitress?"

I shake my head.

"James was staying in Belgium for a long weekend when he struck up a conversation with a local waitress. Pretty thing apparently, very petite. But when he asked if she would like a drink and she politely declined, rumour has it that he lost it. Completely lost it. 'You only spoke to me so you could enjoy rejecting me!' he shouted. And apparently, though I don't know if this is true – he broke her jaw."

"James broke a woman's jaw? Are you sure?"

"No. Not at all," he replies, exhaling. "It's just a rumour, but a rather detailed one, you must admit. Look Vincent, be careful with him tonight. I'm speaking in terms of you and Carina. Don't pay her too much attention. If James sees the two of you exchanging glances, we might all get to see his volcanic temper. I get the sense he is just about keeping a lid on it but Carina's presence is putting him on edge, I can see that. Be careful."

I nod. Footsteps suddenly become audible in one of the parallel hallways and Graham hurries me down the stairs. He nods to Francoise out on the patio.

As we move outside my attention is arrested by the ice sculptures, which are now starting to melt into a pool of silver. The mist emanating from them has built into a translucent cloud. In their state of disintegration they now seem more realistic portraits of their subjects, and all the more beautiful for the decadent air that they give off. I catch a glimpse of a woman's figure moving between them, but think I should dismiss it as drink-induced. But then I make out that strange motion again, a figure weaving meditatively through the sculptures, and it strikes me. Elise is down there.

"I was wondering where you've been," I call, walking

towards the mist. The movement stops for a moment and then resumes, as if the figure has dissolved into the cloud. "You keep disappearing."

I run towards the statues, flail quickly towards the moving shape to catch it. But as I level with the statues I see it is not Elise between them at all. It's Carina.

"I keep disappearing?"

"Sorry, I thought – I thought you were someone else."

"You did?" She stands still, and with her unique air of slightly bruised confidence I wonder how I ever mistook her movement. Perhaps I knew it was her all along. Perhaps I tricked myself. That's what I told myself at the time.

"I don't know who I mistook you for." I step around the statue of Barbara as Carina resumes her movement. I see now that it is a slightly drunk, faltering dance that she is conducting as she cradles a glass of champagne in one hand. It seems tonight is affecting each of us in very different ways, revealing how we each deal with unusual situations.

I want to speak naturally with her, but can't find a way to penetrate that cloud. I am so used to her feeling distant from me. For so long both of us have managed to stay intimate, while also keeping one another at an arm's length. But now the trick of the mist has drawn me into her, and I am not sure if I should escape.

She opens her mouth as if to speak, but instead cocks her head to one side and bites her bottom lip. I look back to the house, to the gold silhouettes just visible within it, and wonder if I should go inside. But I know that I won't forgive myself if I do.

"Your statue looks so serious." She leans round to it, swinging on Barbara's elbow. "Does this statue suggest that she sees you as a critic?"

"I think this statue suggests that she sees me as gay."

"Then what," Carina says, swinging round to the elegant sculpture of herself, "could this possibly say about me?"

"I don't know." I consider the statue of Carina. It depicts a ballerina in flight, holding a pose which seems to defy gravity. Carina appears in the mist behind it, smiling curiously. The mist seems to have distilled on her face, giving it a pale sheen that for a moment makes her resemble another statue. "I don't know," I say again. "Perhaps it alludes to some flamboyant temperament that you keep hidden?"

She doesn't smile, but slips a slender arm over her statues shoulder. She pouts next to its face. She seems more playful than usual; I wonder if it is the drink. That would explain her dancing alone, outside, with a series of ice sculptures. "She's prettier than me, isn't she?"

"No she isn't."

"Well she's certainly more flexible. That's not a pose I have been able to pull off for quite some time."

"Then tonight is the night to try," I venture, setting down my drink. She smiles. "Put down your glass Carina. If you need me to show you how to pull off this move, then that's just what I'll have to do."

She laughs brightly, and considers herself. Then she flicks a foot forward and with flashing eyes raises the hem of her dress above her knees. Slowly, like a swan dipping into a pool, she eases up her back thigh and gradually extends her leg. Her sudden focus, her sudden professionalism, is really quite attractive.

"Thank God you didn't need me to do that," I whisper.

"I'm not there yet," she says, her Spanish accent suddenly distinct. "It still hurts at this point."

I pass alongside her leg, and gently lift her knee a little higher. "Does that hurt?" I ask.

She pauses. "No, that helps. I'm sure it can still be done."

I gently squeeze her knee, feeling a pulse run through me as I take in the scent of her body. Up close the combined effects of her movements are overwhelming, and I wonder if a woman's body has ever had such an effect on me. "Slightly higher," I murmur. "And you have to look more serious when you do it."

Carina winces as I ease her knee a little higher, and then something in her body seems to click. "I think I'm there," she says, holding the pose.

"I think that's it," I say, and we both start to laugh, out of synch. This makes us laugh more.

She straightens up, jumping a few times with happiness. "I didn't make it look easy, did I?" She laughs, "but I did it."

"You didn't make it look unfamiliar," I answer.

"That makes me feel better than any drink. Come on." Then Carina takes my hand and pulls me into the mist.

"Where are you taking me?"

"You'll see."

The summer house looks crooked and spectral, as if it came straight from the pages of a fairy tale. It looks as if we have caught it pulling off some strange pose that it now has to hold for the duration of our visit. Carina holds my hand as she leads me up its wooden steps, to the dilapidated bench on its porch.

We peer within its windows. Inside we can just about make out rocking chairs and a maypole, the multi-coloured ribbons now faded. I wonder if these objects were left by the previous owner and if so what they reveal about his life. "Something tells me Francoise has preserved this summer house exactly from our last visit," Carina whispers. "You see – there's the champagne bottle that we drank on the lawn."

"Why would she do that?"

"Francoise has these pet little obsessions, doesn't she? And I suspect we are one of them."

We sit on the bench, and for the first time our rapport starts to feel unbridled.

"She did make a rather pointed reference to the two of us in her reading."

"That's not what I meant," she replies. "I meant that The Intimates are an ongoing obsession of hers."

"Oh."

"Although I think you might be right. I've always wanted to be like Francoise, but was never any good at being manipulative. My mind is full of these vague preoccupations, and she always has an agenda. Her reading made me think about the signals we unwittingly give off to our friends though."

"Are you talking about us now? I should check this time."

"Yes, I'm talking about us now."

"And do you think her portrait of you then was accurate?"

She flashes a glance at me, looks down. "I think that other people can sometimes see things about you that you don't see yourself, yes." I feel my heart lift and I instinctively try to move closer to her, but the arm of the bench stops me. "Did you think her reading was effective?" she asks.

"Effective? I think it has made us see ourselves in a new light. It certainly reminded me of the ambitions I had when I was young, and what became of them. I realised that you never see yourself in focus, as you obscure your own vision."

"Her little speech made me understand the egotism of youth," she replies. "She accurately portrayed me as someone with an underlying sense of entitlement. At that age I was sure that fate would take a hand in making sure all my desires were satisfied. And now I see that the world is more chaotic, and more self-involved than that could possibly allow. I was so arrogant!"

"I think all of us felt that when we were young. It's just that most of us could never have put that into words."

"All those times when you looked at me and thought I was miles away; I was probably just working these things out in my head." She taps her head as she says this.

"Something always told me that we had the same take on things."

"Really? But we never spoke. We should have found

the time to open up to each other. But something always got in the way."

She swings her legs down and steps to the window. I wonder if she's going to try another ballet move, but instead she puts her hands over her eyes and peers within. "Let's go inside." I feel a rush of exhilaration as she takes my hand again.

We have to work to open the door; time has sealed it shut. I try to open it in one faultless, masculine gesture and Carina laughs when I revert to pushing it open with my shoulder. I almost topple inside the darkness when it bursts open, but her hand restrains me.

"This is like stepping into a time portal," she says.

"It's like a Victorian toy box," I answer, composing myself.

The room is lit only by the faint light from the house, which makes each toy look unsettling. Spinning tops lay on their side, as if having drunkenly failed in their ambitions. Dolls houses without roofs reveal their intricate interiors. Carina stoops to inspect them, gasping with wonder at their dusty secrets. She disappears behind a small Punch and Judy theatre, and tries to scare me with a crocodile puppet. Being barely able to see her when she emerges, somehow gives me confidence. It allows me to treat her as the person I tend to in my mind, and as I do so she becomes that woman. We toy with masquerade masks, and I make her scream with laughter when I surprise her with a gargoyle one while emitting what I intend to be a monstrous sound – which sounds more like a weak gargle. She brushes dust from dolls that have long become expressionless. "What is this place?" I ask.

"The owner of this house lost custody of his daughter when his wife left him," she says, putting on a mask. "Francoise told me that he kept this summer house full of toys in the hope that she would one day return. Isn't it tragic?"

"There's something quite melancholy about the whole house. It seems to almost be a monument to irretrievable times."

Carina steps out of the shadows and reveals her face from behind the mask. The two of us spot a large wooden elephant, its trunk coiled triumphantly in the air. Carina claps her hands; we straddle it and face one other.

"I know what you mean about how something always got in the way," I say. "Do you remember the last time that happened?"

Through the darkness, I think I see her smile. She seems tempted to hide her face with the mask again; she holds it inches from her nose. "What night was that?" I wonder if she really knows.

"That night the six of us came to see you dance." She smiles faintly; it seems she's not replayed the memory as much as I have. The mere reminder of that evening seems to make her flinch with caution, and it's a painful sight. She looks at me silently.

"It had been a long time since the two of us had properly spoken. That night I tried to make it happen though, didn't I?"

"I think I can distinctly remember wanting us to talk

properly that night too," she says, raising the mask.

"Do you remember how it happened though? You'd just finished the show and everyone was talking about how exquisite your dance was. Francoise was practically bursting with pride. And you looked so flushed with happiness."

"It did go well," she whispers.

"And on the way home we all walked along the river. It had those gold lights back then, the ones that lined the boulevard right up to the city wall. Something happened that night, which made the two of us fall behind the others. We sat down for a while by the river, looked out at it. I got the sense that something had been unleashed in you during the dance. I think I was hoping to unleash something else as well."

"You said some very sweet things that night Vincent. Things that suggested you'd been thinking about me a lot. That you saw me in a way I had never seen myself. I was worried that you thought there was more to me than there actually was."

"I knew you were worried about that."

The darkness is growing deeper now, but I can sense her moving nearer and further away as the scent of her perfume rises and fades.

"No man had ever spoken to me like that before. No-one had ever said that I could mean that much to them. I didn't think I had it in me."

"You were dating that guy, weren't you? You seemed a little reluctant to hear what I had to say."

"Not reluctant Vincent. Just unprepared – and perhaps a

little overwhelmed. Your feelings were so intense, and you were so clear in expressing them."

"I remember."

"Don't be embarrassed by that."

"I remember that we ended up pinned against each other, lying on the wall we'd been sat on. And we spoke for a few minutes, inches apart from each other. I wondered if I was going to kiss you."

"A little like now?"

"Yes. And I was just wondering if I should kiss you when – "

She laughs. A laugh so resonant and bright that it suddenly dispels any doubt that I've ever had about the two of us. "And then Graham came round the corner, didn't he? Drunk as a lord."

"Drunk as a lord," I whisper. She looks down, and gathers her dress before dismounting the elephant. We trail outside to the silver-lit porch, and sit down slowly on it.

"This isn't easy," she says. Her expression is serious. "For us to talk openly, there are years of cobwebs to part to one side."

"But don't you see? You were right when you talked about the egotism of youth. We believed that everything we desired would come to pass. I've since learnt that sheer bravery is needed to make that happen."

She smiles faintly, as if anticipating something.

"You know what I want to say, don't you Carina?"

"I know that you are probably caught up in the evening."

"It isn't that. When you say the two of us were never

able to speak, you must be aware that isn't true. We've both been afraid to, and so have contented ourselves with circling one another from a distance."

She looks at me, her eyes wide and vulnerable. We draw closer, and my hand rises to touch her cheek. She closes her eyes as it does. I watch, with the precision of a voyeur, as her eyelashes flutter at my touch.

"Don't," she whispers. "We can't. What about Elise?"

"I'm not sure anymore that Elise and I are right for each other." She flashes me that glance again, and closes her eyes as my fingers trail down her neck. And then her body instantly dissolves, slipping beneath me. Her legs part, wrap around me, and as she lies down on the bench I press against her again. I'm not sure if she has suddenly submitted to my need to dominate her, or if this is simply the end of one long movement of intimacy.

"What about James?" she whispers, her lips inches from mine. "He would lose his mind if he saw this. Vincent, we can't."

"Everything that's happened tonight has told me that we must." But I can see fear moving backwards and forwards behind her eyes, like waves that can't be quelled.

I wonder if Carina's mysticism can be explained by this motion behind her eyes, whether for a long time she has been locked into a reverie by it. I see how hard it will be to quell that rhythm; that I must not try to suppress it but instead shape my expressions to merge with it. I know I will then propel myself into those waves, to be tossed and banded at the mercy of long-restrained emotion. The desire to give myself completely to her comes with the realisation that I do strongly believe we must be together.

This realisation extends into the sweep of my hand onto her fine skin, which settles and troubles her with such brutal synchronicity. Those long awaited, finally realised moments tremble from me as if sourced from the essence that we so rarely reveal. I think I am caressing her to part the waves of doubt that have washed backwards and forward behind her eyes for years. I wonder if I have the strength to do it, if I have the strength to also face my own future. But as the stroking continues – incessantly, rhythmically, with a sensuousness almost ill-fitting for such a gesture – I finally believe I can assure her until she calms. And I'm sure Carina also senses that resolve, that she is aware her own desires are played upon her skin like open nerves that I'm soothing. The trembling in her eyes suggests the sudden, overwhelming knowledge that I can settle all of her doubts. And in this moment of near clair-voyance I feel something move in her face. She parts from me.

"What about James?" she says. "And Elise? There are too many other people to consider before we can cause this pain." She rises to her feet, stroking the back of her hair as if to recreate my movements.

"Are you saying you won't give us a chance?"

She looks away from me. "I want to Vincent, I want to so much. But how can I be sure it is the right thing to do?"

"Carina, I feel tonight as though I've been given a second chance. I've learnt that I must seize the opportunity to have the life I want, even if it means confronting my father." She looks at me, as if frightened in advance.

"I'm asking you to face what is right for you in the same way, if it is us being together. You said yourself that our hidden desires do not naturally come to light; we have to push for them to be satisfied. That is what I am doing now. Even if we agree to try, we have no guarantee that will be enough; but we must try at the very least. If we don't, both of us will continue to spin through the world with no direction, unable even to relate to ourselves."

"I don't know if I'm strong enough to do that," she says, suddenly looking resolved. "My dancing was more important to me than anything, and fate took it away from me. It took it despite the fact that it was the only thing that made sense to me, despite the fact that without it I've been trapped in a world without meaning. I'm afraid I'm not able to put my faith in fate again Vincent. If we're together, I will also have to face James, and everything about him that utterly terrifies me. It will mean the end of our group, you know that, don't you? The group that has held us together for so long."

"That has held us back."

She nods, looking back at the house. Her expression is the same as the one that darkened her face when she tried to mimic the Turkish dancer. I realise that I cannot expect someone to swallow pain that I have never experienced.

"We should go back inside," she whispers. "We should go back and join the rest of them. If you want to?"

"Yes, I do," I say, with some reluctance.

We step down from the summer house and walk slowly back into the mist. As it gradually thins, revealing the lights of the house, I start to count every step. Carina moves wordlessly at my side, and I wonder if she knows that by counting I'm trying to preserve the sensation of being at her side for as long as I can.

Francoise is waiting with pursed lips at the door, as if she's also been measuring the length of our conversation. "A drink, Carina?" she says, giving me a knowing smile as she opens the door for us.

James is lingering on the patio, and looks as though he has been pacing up and down. From a distance I wonder if he is smoking, but as I approach him I see that he is clasping his fist to his mouth and blinking hard. It is only as I draw up to him that I see he is also breathing fast. As I get closer he begins to turn away from me.

"Are you alright?"

"Is that Vincent?" he asks, his pale eyes passing blankly over me. A trembling smile plays upon his lips.

"Yes, it's Vincent." I wonder how he was able to guide himself so precisely through the library and yet be so slow to recognise me. I wonder if it's a trick, but then berate myself for my cynicism. He is shivering violently, and as I draw near the fist flies back up to his mouth.

"James, you're a quivering wreck. What is wrong with you?"

"Vincent, your father is here."

I pause.

"You must be joking."

I look inside the French windows. I can see the backs of The Intimates, huddled in a cautious semi-circle, their immobile bodies' suggesting gazes fixed on a focal point.

I hear nervous laughter, and Francoise's face presses against the window, gauging my reaction.

"He'll know you're here now," James says. "You have to go in, right now. Don't let him come back outside Vincent."

"I'm not going in until you're okay." I know it's an excuse. I know I'm the last person qualified to comfort him. But I'm desperate not to go inside. Not after that conversation with Carina, not yet. I want to preserve the feeling of it, but as ever he has arrived to deny what I might otherwise have savoured.

"I just need some fresh air Vincent, I'll be fine."

Inside, I curse him for not needing me to stay. "Did he say something to you?"

He nods, and again begins to press his fist against his mouth. I have never seen him like this before; his body seems gripped by an escalating, almost hysterical reaction.

"It's a nervous tick. I get it when I'm nervous."

"What did he say to you?"

"He said, 'Still playing the disabled fool? How many fingers am I holding up?' and his stupid crony found it hilarious."

"Anthony is here with him?"

"Yes. I can see, you know that, don't you? It's just shades of grey. All shades of grey." He bows his head and shakes it, sadly at first, and then ferociously.

"James, take some deep breaths. He isn't worth getting this distraught about."

"And so I said that he was holding up two fingers, because I could see that he was. 'Not so blind after a couple of drinks then?' he said, and him and Anthony laughed. God, I despise that man."

I put my arm around him, and the shaking starts to subside. "James, he's just a sad little bully. He'll never be half the man you are."

He nods, and fishes for a handkerchief which he slowly pulls to his mouth. "You should go in now." A shiver passes through my body. Nonetheless, I feel compelled towards the French windows.

Francoise is waving me inside from them. She looks eager, and I loathe her voyeuristic excitement. I uncoil my hand from James' shoulder and move towards her.

Inside my father is leaning against the dining table, gesticulating to his audience. In his hand is a tumbler that I can see has recently been drained. He looks more pointed and muscular than I remember him being. Standing next to him is Anthony, whose face is already unmasked with appreciation at everything my father says.

As I open the clasp of the door the guests stop moving and turn to face me. Gathered in a semi-circle around my father, he holds the assured pose of someone with everyone's attention. The guests fall into silence; some of them look up.

I notice Barbara and Georgina are not amongst them, but the rest of us are there. They look back at my father, gauging his reaction as I step calmly inside. The room still bears the evidence of dinner earlier, and for a few moments my eyes take in the empty wine bottles, the dirtied plates and the ruffled air of the room. All seem silent and poised, reverent even. Then all eyes turn to me.

"Can I get you anything to eat Sean?" Francoise asks, her gaze passing steadily over to him. He raises his head, his expression finding me but ignoring her.

"Have I disrupted this series of clandestine little chats you are conducting?" he asks.

"I was talking with James, father. He seems a little upset."

"He isn't as frail as he pretends to be. I see your friends are still playing you like a fiddle then?"

"Oh Sean, be kind," Francoise says. The tone of her voice comes as an unexpected balm. "Have some wine; let's not stand around like statues. Walter – some music please. This is a party, let's not forget."

"It's a party alright," I whisper. I make out Graham, standing close to my father, as if anticipating stepping between us. I try to make out his expression, but his eyes don't meet mine. For once his features are indecipherable, even to me.

"It's more like a group therapy session than a party," Anthony says, turning to my father with a small laugh. When my father doesn't respond he throws port down his throat in one aggressive move. "Vincent, you look pale. Are your friends weighing you down?" He laughs at my father who smiles, as if trying to hide his amusement at this.

"Francoise tells me each of her beloved Intimates have an ice sculpture carved in their image," my father finally says. "Georgina's is acting, and Graham's is mid-operation. But I struggled to find out what you were doing in yours."

"Vincent's statue was the hardest to commission," Francoise says, her voice wavering a little. I've never seen her nervous before, or weighed by a sense of expectation. "He's still a developing picture, your son."

"He is rather old to still be developing," he mutters. Graham reacts to this, as if smarting on my behalf. I know better. I know that I must keep my reaction hidden from him.

"I'm getting the sense that Vincent and his father need to be left alone for a few minutes," Francoise declares. "Everyone, shall we go through to the drawing room?"

A few people look at me, before reluctantly starting to disperse. Graham, however, stays.

"To what does everyone owe this honour then?" I ask.

He looks at Anthony who nods as if allowing him to proceed. "You parted from me on bad terms Vincent."

"We parted from one other on bad terms. You treated Elise abominably."

"I didn't treat her at all," he says, with a wan smile that he extends towards Anthony.

"I think that Vincent is wondering if you came here to apologise," Graham says. His voice is defiant and shrill, and I feel very grateful for his boldness.

"Still hanging out with the queen then?" he replies, not looking at Graham.

Graham straightens up, and inhales slowly.

"Still having your little daydreams indulged by the spooks that you hang out with?" he continues.

Anthony laughs, unashamedly. "Spooks" he repeats. He

looks at my father, and their eyes meet as they smile at one another.

Graham's face creases, as if suppressing something. Words rise up in my throat, to counter this insult to my friend, but my mouth just unhinges wordlessly. My father presses his advantage as I step back. There's now a note of triumph in his voice.

"You've spent too long prolonging these disagreements between us Vincent. If you're not prepared to apologise to me here then you will come home now so that we can sort this out man to man."

"These people are my friends. They are not spooks," I say slowly.

"Have you not outgrown them Vincent?" His face is red now, flushed with emotion. Graham looks at him.

"These damaged little creatures, soothing each others' petty little wounds. Do you not think you should probably sever ties with them and start to build yourself a career now?"

"We haven't discouraged him from doing anything," Graham says.

"Tell that little *fairy*," my father booms, his face turning to Anthony, "that either he leaves or I do. I am not prepared to suffer contributions from that fag."

Anthony cocks his head, as if considering the vile comment reasonable. "Quite."

"Pray, how have I prohibited you from anything other than laziness?" my father asks.

"You misinterpret anything I do that is not in line with your wishes as laziness. You have treated my efforts to take up writing with nothing more than disdain." The words are out before I have considered them, and they feel horribly raw.

"*You* can't make a living as a writer Vincent. If Anthony here can't do it, then you certainly can't. You have to pick a profession, like a real man."

"No," I say, surprised at my assertiveness. "I can follow my own ambitions, and not those handed to me by you. If you think I lack the talent that is not my problem. If you came here to tell me yet again that I am wasting my life then you are wasting your time."

"Your impertinence astounds me." Setting his glass on the table and stepping forward. I instinctively step back. "I look at you, and I see that you are barely out of your swaddling clouts. An impertinent child, that is what you are; your head lost in a cloud of vague ambition. And yet you scold me, your loving father, who tries to guide you from your wilderness. Anthony, do you see what I have to put up with? From my only son?"

Anthony nods sagely.

"I am trying to save you from embarrassment, from humiliation. That is all; is that such a terrible cause for a father to take up?"

I pause to rally my words, aware of how articulate I now must be. Finally the words come.

"From now on, I am not going to let you stop me." I speak quietly, but the words are clear and resonant. Graham raises his head, and for a moment I think I see some pride in my friend's eyes.

"This is ridiculous," Anthony whispers, stroking his hair.

"You're right," my father says. "What he just said was *quite* ridiculous."

"You know I have it in me too, and it frightens you." My voice is shaking now, but mercifully it's still distinct. "It suits you that I am the idiot son and you are the mighty father, so wrongfully ignored."

"You can't write Vincent. You don't have the *ability*," he hisses.

"I'll show you that I can," I answer, my voice so faint that it almost cracks. The voice I continue with is one that comes from my very essence, the one that has been suppressed for many years. "I will show you that I have enough talent to be reckoned with. And then perhaps the two of us can make amends."

The words hang in the air. I feel proud to have put them out there. I feel as though I have used Franz's advice, fed off my father's negativity and turned it into something powerful and real that could now alter my life for the better.

He looks up, but the usual scorn in his expression seems to be missing. "I am not going to stand around and have my support insulted in front of these strangers," he proclaims, gesturing to Graham. "You are coming with me Vincent. Your mother would be astounded at your insolence, but there is still hope. You and I can make amends if you leave with me now. We are going home."

I look at Graham, whose expression pleads at me.

"Vincent, get your coat. We are going," my father says again.

I step towards him. Graham stands up straight, his face

turning slowly to my father. "He is not going with you. He's staying here, with his friends."

My father turns to look at him, with a frightening leer in his eyes. "Are you *still* talking to me?"

"Don't you *ever* speak to him like that again."

My father looks quickly at me. "Are you coming?"

"No," I answer, my voice hot and dry. "I'm staying."

He stops for a moment, looks at me. His lips curl in rage, as if I have just overstepped a mark. Anthony folds his coat over his arm, considering me with a suddenly different expression.

"You are not leaving yet Sean," a voice says, and as Anthony steps back I see Barbara and Georgina standing in the doorway.

"Barbara?"

"Can I intrude upon this reunion for a moment?"

Her makeup looks a little smeared, and her hair more tousled than I remember it being. Georgina has a calm expression on her face, and she doesn't look at me as the two of them enter the room, the door closing quietly behind them.

"This is a private discussion," Anthony says.

"This is between me and my son Barbara. Perhaps you should just toddle away."

"No." Barbara's voice is pronounced and determined; completely different from its usual coquettish lilt. "I think there is something that Vincent and Georgina need to know. And this time you are not going to stop me from saying it."

"Barbara, do not make a spectacle of yourself,"

he counters.

I can't bear to look up at my father. I suddenly can't bear to look up at all.

"I am going to speak, Sean, and the two of you are going to listen." Her voice is shaking, so much that it is barely perceptible. My father looks suddenly very uncomfortable. He leans back.

"Georgina knows," Barbara says, her face tilted in his direction. As I look up I can just about make out her strained face leaning into his bowed head, as if she is about to weep. "And if Francoise has been as loose with her tongue as I suspect she has, Vincent knows too. And this time – " her voice falters as she speaks, and my father raises a finger to his lips. "This time," she continues, raising a finger back, "you can't threaten me with anything."

The five of us stand for a moment, our expressions fixed to the floor. And then all eyes fall to my father.

When Barbara plays out her story she does so carefully and emotionally. It echoes Francoise's earlier confession almost to the letter. As it unfurls I see a gradual change in my father that surprises me. He stands mute, as if it is requiring great endurance merely to listen to her. But gradually her words start to unnerve him. The sheen on his forehead starts to glisten, and he begins to lean against the dining table as if requiring its support just to stay upright. By the time Barbara has finished, his pose has changed completely. He looks distant, as if her words have somehow winded him, but determined to not reveal that. We have all turned towards him now, and I sense that in doing so, each of us are predicting his impending response. But a response doesn't come. There is just an enormous, enveloping silence, and the slow rasp of Anthony's breath as he inhales and exhales inches from my father.

Georgina and I exchange shocked, placatory glances. My father looks sideways at Barbara but she remains defiant, her hands clasped to her hips.

As my father draws a deep breath his eyes confer with Anthony. But on this occasion even Anthony does not have a stinging remark to draw from his repertoire. He stares apologetically at my father, who finally looks up and nods at their coats, thrown over the dinner table. Reluctantly the two men move over to them. Every movement is amplified as my father coils the coat around his arm, the fabric bristling in my ears as it crumples. Anthony watches over him, but my father does not look up; he now seems unable to look anyone in the eye. We watch as the two of them gather their coats, turning to leave with a distinct lack of ceremony. He doesn't glance at me as the two of them exit the room, leaving behind a gaping silence that I can't imagine fading.

From the patio Francoise looks through the French windows as she watches her two guests leave. But clearly she has no intention of going after them. Her pose is one of gentle satisfaction, and I feel a sudden warmth towards her. Graham, Georgina, Barbara and I move silently outside.

"He was not expecting anyone to stand up to him,"

Francoise says, with a small note of contentment in her voice.

"I'll be in touch with him soon," I reply. "To let him know how I'm getting on. I've still not given up hope that one day the two of us will see eye to eye."

"Very wise," she says. "You're right to think that may yet be a possibility. But most of all I am glad that Barbara got to say her piece."

Barbara smiles at her.

"I have no idea why you thought it would be a good idea to invite my father here tonight. But now that I've confronted him, I feel grateful that I had the chance to do so. I thought I probably never would – and that if I did, I would waste the opportunity."

"You underestimated yourself," Francoise says, curling her arm through mine. We all look to one another for comfort, now that the situation has dispersed. I want to tell Barbara that I admire her for having the courage to face up to a man so capable of viciousness. But it seems like she's in a state of reverie, as if she is replaying the last few minutes in her mind and savouring her sense of triumph. I deem it too soon to speak to her, and that Francoise feels the same. Barbara smiles at Francoise, and as she does a ripple of relief passes over us. Francoise smiles back, perhaps satisfied that her manipulations have been vindicated. "Now come on," she says, motioning with her arms. "This is a party."

Franz, Carina and Elise are waiting by the fountains as we move near to them. "I sense that Sean and Anthony have left the grounds," Franz announces, holding aloft a bottle of red wine. We laugh. "Our hostess has achieved her mysterious aims, and it now looks as if there will be no acts of murder tonight."

"How anyone could ever doubt me is quite beyond my comprehension," Francoise replies.

Elise loops her arm through mine, looking relieved to see me. "I feel this evening as if I have met your family for the first time."

"I'm sorry I've spent so much of the evening away from you," I answer. "It's just been so long since we've all been together."

"You'll pay me back for it yet. Look, Francoise gave me a brooch. Isn't it beautiful?" She shows me the compact, glistening jewel clasped to the hem of her gown. It looks to me like a genuine antique diamond, the light from the French windows illuminating it as she turns to me.

"Elise, I think that is real," I whisper, looking over to Francoise.

"I'm very sure that it's real," she replies, laying her head on my shoulder. "Perhaps Francoise is too drunk to realise, but I'm too sober to tell her."

I look over at Francoise, as she offers champagne to her suddenly relieved guests. Something tells me that she knows very well that the diamond is real.

Love's *A House Is Not A Motel* chimes from speakers positioned around the fountains. The silver flumes look poised, resolved against the black sky. Francoise is laughing gleefully as she dances, pouring out champagne for James.

Someone turns the music up and at once all of the bodies

seem to throw off their shrouds. Colour passes into the exposed flesh of the women in their stylish dresses, as Graham and James hoist their arms into the air and spill champagne over one another.

Georgina is dancing a salsa step in the water, flinging water from the tail of her dress as she swings it around her legs, smiling unselfconsciously as Franz and Elise applaud her. She shakes her hips, making Franz howl in delight over the chattering drums. Lilting Latin guitars fill the night sky. Soon, I'm dancing in the pool of the fountain with them, watching Francoise click her fingers above her head as the music builds to a crescendo. The blood in me stills as I see Carina stepping into the pool, biting her bottom lip as she pulls a lock of black hair behind her ear. She seems to throw off her caution, dancing, swinging her shoulders to the beat, her hair shimmering as she struggles to contain an infectious smile. Graham is pushing me towards her as she looks up at me, her mouth opening. Francoise's dogs are flying through the water, kicking up a spray around us, galloping around in tiny circles, barking joyously. All this commotion turns the black water into a mess of droplets and waves; the moon passes milky ripples over the surface. Everyone applauds and screams as my glass is refilled by a butler; alcohol burns in my neck, incense fills the air. Francoise's hand, slim and warm passes around my shoulders, and I kiss her ringed hand, smiling when she spreads her arms out. Fireworks erupt in the sky, blossoming into scarlet and orange bulbs, lighting our spectral faces before fading into the dark. They define everyone, before we slip into

my body and drawing me into her dancing flesh. The colours in her skin are revealed by moonlight and laughter. I capture for a second that fugitive Mediterranean essence of hers, I can almost taste it. I want to dissolve into that fragrance, and she is so gentle and sure. The fountain seems to hold something more vibrant than the rest of the world as we dance. We fling drops of black water over each other; watch them trail down our bodies like beads of sweat. I'm lost as her hands touch my sides, the sheer pleasure of living rolls through my body and cascades out of my fingertips and now she is looking back at the water as if she is dancing with her own shadow. It feels so good to hang onto each second, to let each instant trail and fade in reckless anticipation of the next and the full bodied way you seize it, the way you twist on its wave, spreading your body even as it breaks in those rare seconds that seem so potent you are sure they will never end, those flashes when you give into the surges of the flesh.

As she smiles her expression turns ghostly white as another firework erupts over our heads. While we are dancing together each moment burns with a furious ecstasy. It seems so obvious then that everything will be alright, that every instant from now will distil into a sequence of shivering moments that will fly from our fingertips like the water around us. I hold this belief firmly in my hands for a few seconds, and I clench it tight until it begins to trickle out. Carina looks up at me as the song ends and I wonder if she's held my smile, her face slightly askew, looking at me with curious interest. Suddenly her face lights up, garish and beautiful as a Catherine Wheel spins to life beside us.

I see an expression of pain thrown across her features and I promise myself to remain with her from now on, whatever happens. I resolve to whirl around with this new sense of possibility until everything falls perfectly into place. Then the light from the wheel dissolves away, the willows fade to black, her face darkens and the memory ends.

We carry the rhythm of the song in our movements as we all step into the drawing room. I approach that elegant, high ceilinged room with a kind of awed reverence, as if approaching a grave garnished with decaying flowers. To me the empty wine bottles, the crumbs of cheesecake on the plates and the chipped champagne glasses are all decorations at the graveyard of the party. They're like ghosts, stuck at the site of their demise. The guests similarly stay in each other's orbit, restrained by the circular comforts they offer each other. In my eyes they too are defined only as a larger category and yet are unable to gift rejuvenation to their accomplices. It seems that the axes they revolve upon withhold them from their particular destinies. I wonder if people are reluctant for parties to end because their departure severs them from the synchronicity they have forged with their fellow guests. When we are severed from the malnourished umbilical cord of a party each of us are propelled back into the world with no rhythm to now follow except the one that punctuates our anxieties.

The detritus of the party does not disappoint; each of it as hopeless and gorgeous as I would have imagined.

Candlesticks burnt to the root, now turned black from the flames which once lit the hopeful faces of the guests. The plates of shattered tortillas and party streamers, their bright colours now faded. They look to me now like intestines sprawled over delicate plates, decorated with chipped gold italics, charming and forlorn under the warm light from the lamps. And perhaps most mournful of all are those huge wine glasses, once vessels of joy and abandon, now holding the tired lip of wine in their bellies. The red rinse that clings to their side makes it appear as if the remainder of the wine is struggling to escape the glass, before slipping back into its sleeping position having failed, just like us. Just like all the bodies here.

A jazz record quietly burbles from the gramophone as Francoise cradles a wineglass in her fingertips. With her eyeliner streaked and the strap of her dress falling from her shoulder she is a picture of elegant decadence. She catches my eye for a second and then takes up the cigarette at her side. The flame briefly sparks in her gloved hand and then slips into a small orange circle between her pastel coloured lips. The considerate look she gives the bodies before her makes me wonder if she has more plans for them yet.

At the start of the night each guest presented a pristine image of themselves. But their veneers started to slip as the small hours revealed the large thoughts. Though their makeup is smeared and their evening dresses are ruffled each are all the more beautiful for it. What can be more alluring than a person who has unfurled enough to reveal their essence? Who really finds a perfectly shored up mind an attractive prospect? Our appearances finally reflect how abandoned each of us are, languishing in the company of the similarly trapped. Each of The Intimates possess talents that have been mercilessly denied expression. And each of us has since started to twist in themselves – some, like James, have started to convulse.

The momentum of the party has faltered. We exchange glances at one another but remain mute. Perhaps it's the incessant gush of the fateful fountains outside, but this silence terrifies me, and as our hostess Francoise seems culpable for it. A hostess is lauded not just for what she offers, but for what she restrains. When the momentum of a party slows we are each offered a frightening glance at ourselves; frightening because we have began to unfurl. At such moments I see that even in the company of others we are isolated. The loneliness one feels at a party is almost existential in its ferocity, as a party is an occasion specifically designed to prevent that possibility.

I realise then the illusory quality that any good party has. It must briefly convince us that the vaulting emptiness outside our window is not real. It must make us forget the bitter aftertaste of solitude that lingers behind every mouthful of life. But somehow we're never able to forget that silence is always waiting. We grip onto people to dance with, seize people to open up with, all the time not daring to look over our shoulder. The party will inevitably end; and even if the relationships within it do not, new silences will be carved within them in time. But gazing amongst these faces I see that none of that matters. That illusion is essential to our sanity, because in moments of companionship our voids are forgotten. Never are they dismissed more heartily than when we laugh; then even existence winks into insignificance. That emptiness is nothing to be feared; it is what makes us urgently grip onto our companions. We sit in silence, and for those few moments I feel sure that we each belong together.

"I like this song," Carina says, as a new record starts.

"Then we must dance to it!" James replies, his voice slurring. As he rises, his glass slips through his fingers and onto the floor. He staggers loudly into the dessert trolley.

"James, I fear you are too drunk to dance, my friend," Graham says. He rises to take Carina's hand. "Would you permit me to take this dance with her instead?" he asks.

"A pleasure," answers Carina, easing to her feet.

James composes himself, dabbing a streak of red wine on his shirt. "She's rejecting me," he says, as they begin to dance.

"She is not rejecting you." Georgina replies.

"I asked her for a dance, and she turned me down," he insists, moving to meet her eye. Georgina waves her hand dismissively. Elise leans over to whisper in my ear.

"Meet me in the bedroom, two floors above here in a couple of minutes." Her eyes are wide and conspiratorial. A moment later she stands up, and smoothes her dress. "Excuse me for a few moments."

James is watching as Carina and Graham gently waltz through the room. "You'll give James the next dance, won't you Carina?" Georgina asks her. But Carina's eyes are closed; she seems lost in a reverie. I watch them step into one another for a minute, and then set my glass down before leaving the room.

On the way up the stairs I see a flash of red in one of the rooms and wonder if I've caught a glance of Elise. But then I hear the unmistakeable sound of Franz's voice, low and placatory.

"I'm sure I heard someone move," a female voice whispers, in response to him.

As I quickly pass the door that the sounds emanate from I catch a glimpse of Franz pressed against Barbara, whose dress is hitched up to reveal her black stockings. I quietly press on up the stairs before either of them has seen me.

Elise throws her scarf around my neck and pulls me into a side room. She seems driven by some new passion; lust or jealousy. Usually I have to earn intimacy with her, but this time she's charged with a sharp new motivation. I can still smell Carina's perfume on my jacket, and by thinking of her I allow her to enter the room too. She becomes the third person many couples suppress in memory or threat. I've never known Elise be less sensual than when she throws me against the window, before letting go of the scarf with one hand. The window's still open and I almost fall through, but then that scarf loops over my head and draws me back towards her.

Shadows cast by the figures outside flash against the opposite wall. They crowd behind Elise as she steps closer, her lipstick now resembling a streak of blood. She pushes me against the window frame, her lips flashing across the room. As her tongue clamours into my mouth I feel that dizziness return. My mind is still dancing in the fountain, that feeling has barely started to recede from my limbs. I know this should be the climax of the evening but all I can think of is the flying water and Carina's strange, nervous movement. These nights preserve their wonder in strange moments, but never in ways you'd imagine.

Would Carina struggle to open my shirt and kiss me passionately, with a tongue I barely respond to? Would she tear at my clothes with a steely smile? She would surely lie beneath me, she would twinge slightly as if I'd hurt her when we made love, she'd look pale and sensual afterwards wrapped in the sheets. She would look at me with vague eyes and smile only faintly when I reached for her. I try to pretend it is Carina's mouth that smothers my neck with kisses, that it is Carina who gives away her flesh so easily, persuading herself from her dress. Elise pushes me over with one hand, and I trip backwards onto the bed. As she towers over me she starts to wind her neck scarf around one fist.

"Does this mean that I finally have your attention?" she asks, coiling it tighter. I wriggle like a nervous animal, and with flashing eyes her teeth find my neck. Her mouth meets mine, and when she bites my lip her teeth draw a little blood. She parts from me, a strap from her dress falling to her elbow.

"You've been playing a game with me tonight, haven't you? I'm old enough to know when I'm being toyed with, and that's exactly what you've been doing. Now I'd say that it's my turn, wouldn't you agree?"

She doesn't see me cautiously nod, trying to push a

playful smile onto my lips. Her head is bowed, her features lost in darkness. She relentlessly winds the scarf around one fist, then lets it slacken before winding it around the other. I feel my heart beat faster; I try to stand up properly against the window sill. "Don't make it harder on yourself. You've had your fun – all evening. If I'm going to now have my fun I think it's only fair that we do things my way, don't you?"

She flashes forward and kisses me with such force that I almost topple through the window. I lose my footing and clamour for the window frame with one flailing hand, but she bats my arm away and makes me fall to the floor. I'm completely at her mercy. She loops the scarf around my neck and pulls me back up, kisses me again. As she does one hand snakes through my hair, her first act of tenderness. But I realise she is coiling the scarf around my neck. She breaks off the kiss, her eyes shining wickedly, and the cord tightens around my throat as she holds it taut with one hand.

"I wouldn't move an inch if I were you."

As the scarf tightens, she reaches behind with her other hand, smiling a little as she unzips her dress. The fabric gasps open, she presses her hot flesh against me.

"Take it off me," she whispers, raising both hands with the scarf. Her breath is hot and slightly sweet.

"Not so tight," I say, in a weak voice that just makes her smile.

"Do as you're told," she says, before giving me a taster of how uncomfortable the scarf can be. Air forces its way from my mouth as she yanks it hard, and I choke. For a moment my head dangles between the two ends of the scarf, I imagine it cutting through my neck like a cheese wire and my head toppling to the ground. I recover.

"Look at my body!" The white glare of the moon accentuates every contour of her flesh. Her skin is as ivory white as a statue, but every sexual advance streaks a flash of scarlet across it. "Take off my dress," she whispers, keeping the cord taut.

Trembling slightly, afraid to break the tension with a laugh, I ease the zip to the base of her back. As I do her upturned breasts tear free from the dress, hardening a little as they come towards me. "Keep your eyes on me," she orders, adjusting the scarf.

I badly want to exhale, to take in a lungful of air, but the scarf makes that seem a distant possibility. "If you're going to enjoy looking at my body you're going to have to pay for it, aren't you?" She ensures my vision is consumed only by her. "Now take off the rest of my clothes."

I dare myself to look down; her body barely visible as one of the outside lights switch off. With her thin dress now coiled on the floor, only her stockings and knickers cover her body.

"Do it then," she says, tightening the cord before treating me to a flush of clear air. As my hands tremble towards her I close my eyes, willing myself to act composed.

I know that she has felt under my mercy all evening but kept that hidden. She's showing a controlling, aggrieved side to her character. A side I always knew existed, but tried to ignore. Under pressure I see I have already learnt some of its requirements. I must also now refrain from revealing a sudden sense of submission.

The first rule is that I must not appear afraid. I must act with utter seriousness, and follow her orders to the letter while not showing any signs of weakness. The second is that I must maintain the illusion that I am secretly enjoying myself, as refusal to do so will be interpreted as an insult. It surprises me how quickly a trapped man learns the rules of his confinement.

I reach around her and slowly draw the thin slip of fabric from her waist. "Don't look down," she says, her lips sparkling. "Just take them off." She leans into me as I push the lacy material down her legs, and she bends as I draw them off her feet. Except for her stockings she's now naked – but I still keep my eyes trained on the froth of white I clench in my hand.

"Good. Now you can look at my body."

In the instant my eyes pass onto it, the cord thrashes tight around my neck. I choke, splutter out air, and she laughs gaily. "You liked looking at that, didn't you?" she sings, as my hands reach instinctively for my throat. For the first time I start to seriously wonder how this game will end. "Did you really think you wouldn't have to pay for that pleasure?" My hands clamber for the scarf and touch something wet. The scarf has torn my skin, drawing blood. I wonder if she is purposefully bruising my neck.

I ease my hands around my throat as she laughs again, and I quickly learn that she was right. Seeing her long, exposed body charged me with pleasure; a pleasure soon neutered by the burst of intense pain.

"Lie on the bed." She pulls the cord tight so quickly that

I move over to it in an instant. She climbs onto it, her mouth grazing against my ear as she presses her body against mine. She kisses my cheeks feverishly, her breath hot and fast. "We'll have to keep quiet," she whispers, pressing a finger to my mouth. Her head descends onto my mouth and she kisses me passionately, furiously, as if I finally now have the chance to pay her back.

Elise becomes the man and I become the woman – my role is to accommodate her, to allow her to find the source of her pleasure. Her tongue searches my mouth, her hand clamours through my hair. She presses my lips to her neck and forces them onto her breasts until our bodies lash against each other, keen to forge an urgent bond. I feel my need to please her rise; a need to match my body to her desires, while all the time playing the victim.

She thrashes her body against mine, her hair strokes my chest. She smiles with a pleasure that's uniquely hers. We press against each other until my body craves to join her. She's tricked me, making me lust for something that terrifies me, and in that moment she eases me into her. I feel that sense of relief, but the cord tightens so hard that the room begins to spin. I try to open my mouth, to beg her not to choke me, to try and break the silence of this game. But she pulls harder on the cord, and my head pulls to one side. I feel the wound on my neck widen, the bruising spread. Every inch of air is forced from my lungs as she pummels into my body. The light glares over her stockings and illuminates their crushing rhythm. "You like that, don't you?" she taunts, finally releasing the scarf as my body stumbles for air. "You didn't really think you wouldn't have to pay for it, did you?"

I want to throw her off. I want to just gorge myself on air, but she has no such concerns. To her, those few breaths were a plentiful reward. Her eyes are clenched shut, her lipstick smeared as her pleasure builds to a crescendo. Before, I would struggle not to tear her from me and lay myself against her, but this time she's possessed. I fear the moment my body will react to her fury, and I urge myself to submit. Be passive, I tell myself – just let her win. She twists and thrashes, and her nails embed themselves in my side until they draw blood. It begins to trickle down her fingernails, and her neck scarf falls between her breasts. I seize the opportunity to throw the scarf to the other side of the room. Even though she now has no weapon she continues to thrash against me with complete control. Without the scarf we are now just a man and a woman, but she still has total superiority. And the fact that she knows that makes me feel somehow humiliated. I know then that Elise has got her revenge. And, as if acknowledging that, she clenches her way into a tearing orgasm. I've never heard a woman make a more feral and unrestrained sound as she makes, gripping me in her fingernails. It irreversibly changes me, as if I've somehow now been freed from my role as a man.

Before the flush of blood on her chest has subsided she prises herself from me and lies on the bed. "Take me quickly," she pleads. "Before people catch us."

I hesitate, and try to steady my breath. I can't tell her I feel nothing for her but fear; that I can't imagine dominating her now, under any circumstances.

"What is it?" she asks, her expression full of accusation.

I wait for a few moments, and mentally count my wounds. The skin on my side is torn by her nails, the wound on my neck is bleeding, there's that slightly preserved twist in my windpipe. I know I shouldn't speak. I'll only stagger over words and tear everything apart. Impetuously, she leans over the side of the bed and pulls her crumpled dress against her body. Her scent is smeared all over the bed, but, even overwhelmed by it, my body still doesn't respond. I retract in fear, pull the sheets towards me. As my body feasts itself on air I realise it is still shackled to the girl outside. That I must preserve whatever little I have left for Carina.

"It's Carina, isn't it?" she snaps, reaching down to adjust her stocking. She looks over my shoulder, at the fountain outside. "I saw the way you looked at her. Does she have something I don't?"

"You're being ridiculous," I say, knowing that the difference between them is all I can think of. I desperately want to be articulate, to explain away this sharp alteration of my feelings. But my body is still demanding that I focus only on survival and it seems unable to produce words. I know that even if the words do come, my throat will be unable to deliver them. I look back at her, sensing her anger build with every second that I don't speak.

"It's okay," she says, pulling the dress over her head and zipping it up with one movement. "You feel you have something in common, don't you? It's that stupid book, isn't it?"

I feel my mouth fall open, but it suddenly feels dry. Confusion overwhelms me, as I realise the moment to respond has passed.

"It's not the book."

"If you think she's better than me because you've both *failed* at something then perhaps you are right for each other," she hisses, reaching down to grab her heels. "If I'd known you were bringing me here as some sort of accessory then I wouldn't have bothered."

"It's not that, I brought you here because I wanted you to meet these people who've been a huge part of my life. But I've realised a lot of things tonight Elise. I'm not the person that you want me to be, and I can only pretend that I am for so long."

"How could you have any idea what I want you to be?" she screams, and then her voice drops quickly to a whisper. "I want you to see how ridiculous it is that you feel a bond with these people, particularly that you feel a bond with *her*. If it was going to happen with her, Vincent, it would have happened by now. Do you really think I'm going to hang around and put up with this?"

"I don't expect you to."

"Well I won't stay any longer then. Not for you, not for any of these other failures."

As she towers over me on the bed I know she realises she has gone too far, but I stay silent. "Have you got nothing to say?" I am hit by the full force of what I need to say to her, but prevented from speaking by fear, pure fear at what she might do.

She suddenly looks vulnerable. "Vincent, I thought you were going to propose to me tonight. How stupid is that?"

"Elise, I am sorry. I am so sorry, you do not deserve

this. I brought you here with good intentions, but tonight something has changed, and I don't think we can go on anymore."

"I told Francoise you were going to propose to me, and then she teased me about it."

"She shouldn't have done that. It was wicked of her to do that, but you shouldn't not have presumed that I was going to propose."

"What should I have presumed Vincent? That tonight you would fall for someone else? You humiliated me. Look at what you make me do."

Her hand slaps me, hard across the face, and then with an anguished cry she hits out at me. I fall from the bed, smashing a bedside vase as my head strikes against it. Looking down at the shards of porcelain I see drops of blood.

"I am being honest with you Elise. I don't deserve *this*."

She steps towards me. In that moment I feel sure Elise could do anything. I'm prostrate at her feet. My body is still attached to her, yet quaking in fear at what she might do. She looks to the neck scarf, and an instant later, streaks over to it. I try to stop her, but she grasps it. I retract, back into the shards of broken porcelain under the window.

"Don't do anything stupid Elise. This little game has gone too far." I feel sure at that moment that I have paid my dues to her. I have been choked, cut open, humiliated. My eyes plead with her to see that our balance has been redressed.

She keeps winding the cord round her hand. I grab my shirt from the bed, and move back against the window.

She comes closer, looking down at me with utter pity. She laughs, and it's a very hollow sound. She screams, kicking the shards from the vase into my half-naked body.

I pull them from me, speckles of blood covering one hand.

"I'm going," she says, her voice shaking with emotion. She paces around the bed, grabbing her handbag and stole. "I'm going to leave you to your pathetic little life. Hopefully you'll realise one day that your father is right." She pauses for a moment, as if willing herself to meet my eye, but her trembling head does not raise itself one inch. And then she turns, and storms from the room. I lean back against the wall and close my eyes.

I crouch there for a while, waiting for my heart to steady again. But even with my eyes clenched shut something tells me I cannot relax yet. The window has been blasted open, and the second I look over to it, shouting fills the air. For a dreadful moment I wonder if Elise is berating Francoise as she storms from the house, but then I recognise Georgina's voice coming from the room below. It seems upset, angry, and the shouted reply it provokes seems to be Barbara's. Has Georgina caught her mother with Franz? I crane through the open window, the shadows in the room beneath suggesting pronounced movements.

"Don't make assumptions Georgina. You have no idea what Franz and I were doing," Barbara says.

'Well you weren't *talking* mother; I'm not a child. He was tucking his shirt into his trousers when I passed him on the stairs, and then when I come up here I see you adjusting your makeup. It's perfectly obvious what the two of you were doing. He is half your age mother, closer to mine than yours. You're an embarrassment."

Barbara responds very quietly, with menacing restraint. I lean out further to catch her words. "What is embarrassing, daughter, is how out of your depth you were this evening. Did you not notice that?"

A pause.

"What on earth are you talking about?"

I hear the clatter of cosmetics, the scratching of a hair-brush. "Did you not look around you at any point Georgina? Did you not notice how many achievers there were at the party? Did you not feel even a little out of place?"

There is silence for a moment and then the sound of repetitive pacing. "You don't get it, do you?" Georgina replies. "You have no idea why I brought you here this evening. You just can't work it out for yourself, can you?"

"I don't have time for this."

"Well I'll make the time for you mother. I'll work it out on your behalf. I brought you here tonight because I wanted you to see the effect of that little agreement you parents made all those summers ago. When you all decided to push your little children to each achieve something great. I wanted you to spend just one evening with the people whose lives were wrecked by that decision. You're too pig-headed to look beyond their achievements and glamour; but every one of The Intimates is a ruin. A decaying, crumbling ruin, twisted by self-hatred.

Permanently dogged by the idea of what they *think* they should be. Not people at all; just petri dishes for you to all plop your ambitions inside."

"As usual, I have no idea what you are talking about Georgina. All I know is that everyone here has gifts that they have used to a greater or lesser degree. Everyone except you. Because you have no talent." The final words are whispered in a deadly monotone.

When Georgina replies her voice is raised, slightly hysterical. "You're so pathetic! As if that matters. You're still living in the past. You think you're a movie star, but you were never one in the first place. You were just a piece of cinematic fluff. And yet you carry on like you're Greta Garbo, embarrassing yourself day after day. Can't you see that?"

Barbara is silent.

"Every second of the day you're living this failed dream. When you realised your time had passed you tried to channel your ambitions through me. But then something occurred to you, didn't it? That it would be easier to take all of your bitterness and spite out on your daughter. I can't believe that I brought you here tonight to try and get you to see the consequences of your actions. To try and perhaps mend things between us. That could never happen. You're too pig-headed!"

"How dare you!" Barbara screams, and half a beat later I hear the shattering of glass.

There's a smattering of muffled shouts, the sound of rinsed glass. "Don't blame me if your career is over. Don't you dare blame me!"

Barbara curses something inaudible back. It sounds understated but viciously sharp.

"Let's not go there. *Let's* not go there," Georgina hisses. "Your boyfriend was right, he was right all along. I've read your diary mother. The one you left in the garage? I know what happened."

Barbara seems to have fallen silent.

"Oh yes, you listen to me now, don't you? Because you know that I know the truth. And that is what makes me right, and you wrong about all of this. It was you that let my brother die. You wrote in the diary that you knew very well the au pair would not be experienced enough to handle two young babies. You knew that before you even employed her. And yet you pursued employing her and her alone. And then after only a few weeks she left both of us unattended in the bath – and only I survived it. And yet in your diary you don't express grief, you don't mourn. No, nothing like that. You just mention how much more *manageable* your life will now be. I won't ever know if you planned the whole thing, if you wanted both of us out of your life. But what I do know is that you hired that au pair with your eyes wide open. You knew only too well how inexperienced she was. You knowingly neglected both of us until one of us died. You killed my brother."

The last words are barely completed when the air is filled with a terrible scream, followed by the sound of more shattered glass. Then a sickening thump, as if a body has been thrown against furniture. I hear the trickling of shards, a series of pleas which seem threatening but edging towards apology. "You've – " Barbara starts, and then she screams agonisingly, a scream that turns to an anguished sob as if she's consumed with pain. Has Georgina lashed out at her? Stabbed her?

I realise that I have to intervene. I have to separate them. I have to see if Barbara is alright, to find the source of that terrible scream. I wonder if it is all in my mind, but the awful chill in my blood tells me that it is very real. I stagger to the entrance, look wildly around me for the stairs.

"Barbara?" I fly downstairs, to the room directly below. But it's empty, curtains flying with abandon at the window.

"Barbara!" I shout, wondering if the two of them are perhaps slumped in the corner, but scouring the room I see that it is empty. I tear outside, and a voice catches my ear. It is a short, sharp scream which punctuates the still air.

"Get away from me!" it screams. "Get away from me right now!" It's accompanied by a protestation that's indisputably male.

The sound has come from downstairs, from the library where James and I were, earlier that evening. But as I run in the direction of it, through one of the doorways to my side I see a flash of dark hair that I'm sure is Carina's. Then that male voice again.

"You destroyed me! You rejected me, reduced me to nothing – and now I'm going to do the same to you." There is a sickening curdle to the voice which it takes me a moment to recognise. Finding the room it emanates from I see James, brandishing a large fire poker at a cowering figure in the corner of the library. My blood stops as I see it is Carina. James' other hand is pulling at his belt, his shirt looks unbuttoned. Carina is trembling against a wall of books, her eyes wide with fear. She sees me behind him as I enter the room.

"He's gone mad! He's trying to – he's trying to – "

With Carina's dress torn, and the hand James now has clasped to her thigh, I can see exactly what he is trying to do.

"Don't try and trick me into thinking there's someone there," James leers, taking a step closer to her. "It's just you and me, and I'm going to get what you've been promising me for years."

On a small table by the doorway is a half-empty bottle of champagne. As I grab it James turns towards me with a triumphant leer in his eyes. He swipes the vast poker in my direction, dashing a drinks trolley. I leap back, inches from its terrifying arc. I dash the bottle against the wall and raise its jagged edges at him. The sound of it breaking shocks James, who steps in my direction with the poker. I see now that it's so hot, the tip is glowing.

"Get away from her," I say, as confidently as I can. "Get right away from her James; you're not going to do this."

"Vincent? You have no idea how pleased I am that it's you who's come to her rescue. After all, it's you that has thwarted my destiny so far. Do you not feel even slightly ashamed for all the false advice you have offered me through the years?"

"James come on, this isn't you," I whisper.

"Are you really threatening me with something?" he asks, turning fully towards me for the first time. "I thought perhaps you had accidently broken a bottle, but now I get the impression you are actually trying to threaten me with that little weapon." His whitened eyes shine in the light from the chandelier above. His hair is wild and his shirt open enough to reveal a scarred, naked chest.

"I'm not threatening you with anything. I just want you to let Carina go. Come on James, the poor girl is terrified."

"Poor girl? Your poor girl? She is not yours – she is mine."

Carina screams, tries to wriggle to her feet. James roars in fury and swipes at her with the poker. It tears across a row of books, scorching them in a jagged black line. Some of them start to smoulder as Carina crawls towards me. "Vincent, stop him!"

"Don't you touch her!" James roars.

He raises the poker above his head and smashes me across the chest. I collide with the door in perfect time with Carina's scream. I clutch my chest, doubling over, before thrusting a desperate hand towards the bottle I've dropped. I don't even have time to brace the extraordinary pain as James brings the poker down on me again. But Carina's screaming makes him miss, and he only just catches my neck with its end. As I roll on the floor beneath him, he tears it across the back of my shoulders, and bending over with cautious precision he smashes it again into my chest. A horrible cry emanates from my throat, one of begging rage. My hands tremble for the bottle, finally grasping it and jabbing it in his direction. I need to threaten him with something, something that will frighten him off me. My mind is still with me but my body is now moving much more slowly.

"Leave him James!" Carina cries.

"Come here!" he orders her, as I cower into myself. My head spins; I try to gather composure. As I come to, I see that James is pushing Carina onto the floor, trying to pull off her dress. I launch myself into him and throw him against the bookcase. He raises the poker to swipe me again as I elbow him in the face and his hand opens. Bending over to retrieve the poker I kick him back into the wall of books, and his head catches against it. His body drops unconscious for a few precious seconds.

I grab Carina's hand and pull her behind the wall of books. Too late I realise this hiding place allows him to block our way out. Carina lunges towards a light switch, hoping the semi-darkness will work in our favour.

Leaning against one of the book stacks, we both hold our breath. Carina clutches herself to me. I hope desperately that when he comes to he'll believe we've fled the library. But then through a chink in the shelf I see that James has found his feet, and the poker, and that he is now turning in our direction. His deathly white eyes look possessed.

"Carina, are you in here? I want to apologise. Vincent, let me know if you're in here!"

I see his glazed eyes try to determine shapes in the darkness, and he fumbles towards a light switch that he cannot find.

"Vincent, Carina, tell me where you are. I'm sorry, I was jealous of the two of you. I had a moment of madness." The light comes on, throwing bright colour into the room. With one hand I beg Carina to stay silent, but she lets out a small plea of fear. We hear him move nearer, desperately hoping that she has not given us away. But now James seems to know where we are. The slow rise of his eyes also suggests that he knows he has us trapped.

"Be reasonable, you two," he pleads. "I have seen you both, snuggling up to each other in the summer house, exchanging affectionate little glances. And you Vincent, pretending to be my friend. That wasn't right, was it? Both of you have taken me for a fool for a very long time. Come out now and show yourselves, so we can resolve this once and for all. My temper has subsided, I promise. Let us now be friends."

I count off three, two, one on my fingers to gesture when we should rush to the back of the library, to find an exit there. When I clench my fist the two of us rise to run away. But with a triumphant smile James rounds the corner, appearing at our side with the poker above his head. He swipes me across the back with it, as I crash to the floor. He grabs Carina by the wrist and throws her against a wall, books tumbling all around them. I look up, struggle to my feet. She ducks from his grip but with unerring precision James grabs her wrist and throws her back against the books. I launch myself at him, throwing him against the wall. A shelf of books collapse onto his head, bringing him to the floor. But a second later he is flailing to find his feet.

I grab Carina's wrist and pull her towards the other end of the library. We round bookcases, streaking up and down aisles to try and lose him, the metallic clutter behind us suggesting that James has not only found his feet but also the poker.

"I'm not going to hurt either of you. It was just a moment of madness. Come back here so we can resolve this!" His voice is now a raw scream. Carina runs ahead of me, but as we reach the back wall of the library I realise there is no exit there. We are trapped. The clattering in our direction, followed by his confused shouts, suggests he will be with us in only a few moments.

"Where do we go?" Carina cries, her voice hysterical.

Suddenly I remember. My eyes frantically scan the top shelf. It is on the third anxious sweep that I see it. Ayn Rand's *The Fountainhead*, as shown to me by Francoise. Jumping up I grab the spine of the book and pull it back. In one fluid movement the bookcase opens to reveal the tunnel. Another roar confirms that James is almost upon us, just rounding the bookcase as I propel a startled Carina into the passageway, before tearing the bookcase closed behind us, sealing the entrance just as James throws his body against it. The electric candles within illuminate, revealing the secret passageway.

"What the hell is this?" Carina asks, frantically pulling the tear-streaked hair from her eyes. The musty smell of the tunnel fills my nostrils and I suddenly feel trapped. But we can hear James pummelling against the bookcase and I check quickly that the entrance is sealed, noting with satisfaction that it seems to be.

"It's The Fountains' secret passageway." Taking her hand I guide her into the semi-darkness. I wonder if I am taking her down a dead end. My senses, inflamed by the warmth and the colour of the house, are suddenly dulled by claustrophobia. It invokes a sense of panic, heightened by Carina's clear reluctance to go any further.

"This isn't safe, we don't know where we're going!" she pleads, but then we hear James battering against the entrance.

"There isn't time to argue. Francoise tells me this will take us to the very bottom of the garden. We'll be safe from him down there; he can't open the bookcase because he doesn't know how, and we're not going back outside. It's our only choice."

She shakes her head in fear, but the smashing of James' fists and his wild shouts resolve her. I guide her into the tunnel, wondering if my assertiveness is really so well-founded.

I lead her through the circular, brick lined passageway, lit intermittently by electric candles. It winds in one long crescent into the distance. The two of us, shaking and battered, urge ourselves into the darkness.

"He was trying to touch me Vincent. His hands were all over me." I squeeze her hand harder and start to run with her through the tunnel. It's barely tall enough to accommodate us at full height, and the deeper we go the danker it becomes.

"Francoise told me the previous owner built this in case people came looking for him. We'll be perfectly safe in here," I say, my voice echoing around.

"But didn't she also say how strange the previous owner was? How do we know that he even finished it?" Suddenly I trip on something, and catapult to the floor.

Carina screams, and keeps screaming as she recoils against the wall. I find my feet as she clasps her hands to her face. As I look down I see that I have tripped over a black cluster of cloth and bones that resemble a dead body. A rank stench fills my nostrils. "Carina! Carina, it's okay!"

I bend down to inspect the skeleton of a man, his body clothed in what was once an evening suit, his face pressed into the dirt.

"It's the previous owner." My voice is barely a whisper.

"What?"

"The previous owner. Francoise told me that he built this tunnel in case his debtors came looking for him and he needed to escape, but that one day he disappeared and was never found."

"He must have taken something and then ran inside here," she whispers, pressing her shaking body against mine. At the entrance to the tunnel a clattering is still audible. "Come on," I whisper. "We don't have a choice. We have to get to the other end. We're nearly there." Eventually I see the passageway ending, with the tunnel ascending slightly before merging with a trap door. "That's it, the exit! If what Francoise says is true, we'll now be at the foot of the garden and perfectly safe."

"Thank God," Carina says, holding my hand. "I thought it was never going to end."

I urge her to step back as I find the latch to open the door. Punching against it with my fists, gradually the trap door bursts open, its eroded wooden slats breaking out into the night and revealing above it black sky. "Is there anyone there?" she asks. Her voice echoes around.

Cautiously, I peer through it. No-one's waiting for us; all I see is the dark night, partially lit by stars. I prise myself out of the trap door and onto the grass. Looking around I can see the drained swimming pool just at my side, lit by its interior lamps. I look carefully around me. In the far distance I can see the lights of the house, only just perceptible through the trees. But as I inspect our surroundings more carefully I see that Carina and I are now completely alone. There is nothing in the garden but the pool and the soft hissing of the summer night.

"We're perfectly safe," I say, reaching my hand down to her. "We're by the empty swimming pool at the bottom of the garden."

Carina smiles with relief and holds out her hand to me. I bring her carefully up through the trap door and onto the grass. I seal the door shut, laying a large sculpture over it, just to be sure. "No-one will find us down here."

"Look."

I turn to see what she's gesturing towards. My eyes had missed the seven ice sculptures on the lawn. They now appear to be crouching into the growing pools of water on the grass. They have melted so much that their poses and expressions have been lost. Where Carina's sculpture once danced expressively it now folds into itself; it no longer mocks her for being unable to mimic it. My sculpture now has an expression as glassy as its body. Its limbs are just stumps, dripping onto the grass beneath it.

"Feels liberating, doesn't it?" Carina says. She smiles, and I realise that she is right. Those statues were only able to depict us for a short while before inevitably melting away. But now they've disintegrated we're freed from the constraints that trapped us within. We're now just as amorphous as the water, building into a silver pool at their feet.

Her hand rests on the back of my shirt. "Are you hurt? The back of your jacket has been torn open, it looks a little burnt." I turn to face her. "My God," she says, her face suddenly visible. "He bust your lip open. And your hands… they're bleeding."

"Come on," I say, looking around me and feeling a little less brave. "Let's hide in the pool."

The early morning sun is just beginning to break through as the two of us pick our way through the weeds to the pool. Its lights are clouded over with dust, but the pool is still as illuminated as a rectangular runway. Like two wounded animals we limp towards it in our torn and bloodied clothes, having finally found somewhere to huddle together. We look like two soldiers walking home after a brutal battle, shaken to the core and yet still convinced of our cause. We both seem too shaken to even question why we're going into the empty pool, but it seems now like the one place that can offer us solace. I take off my ripped dinner jacket and place it around her shoulders.

We step carefully down the rusty ladder of the pool, and with one hand I beckon her to join me in its corner. Carina's eyes are alight with the possibility of morning as she lifts the train of her dress, stepping towards me. I crouch in its corner, gratefully receiving her slim body in my arms. I wrap them around her and feel her fingers snake through my shirt, cling to my back. I inhale her scent; it suddenly gives me a kick of strength. I feel like I've chased that scent for a long time, and to have it here with me now helps me relax. I spread out my legs, and she bunches her thighs against my chest. Our two bodies curl together in a desperate state of intimacy. At first I think she is laughing as she lays her head on my shoulder. But then I realise that she's started to cry, out of relief I hope. With the dim air surrounding us our little den is lit up like a cradle, and when her body relaxes in my arms it is as if she finally feels safe.

I smooth her hair and whisper nonsensical words to soothe her. But her sobbing doesn't seem one of grief, it seems wider than that – as if she's weeping about the struggles that continually taint our lives. As I comfort her I feel I am somehow comforting myself, trying to settle everything that's inflamed in my own life. I now see her for what she is – someone unique who's been badly damaged and made to doubt her own ability. Yet she's still preserved the essence that sets her apart. I squeeze her tighter and tell her that she shouldn't cry, that we're both safe now. But I sense it's only with great determination that her breathing begins to settle. Where it was once jagged and broken it now becomes stoical and calm. I feel a sense of satisfaction in having calmed her frightening state of distress.

The last hour has been like a nightmare, and yet those events all seemed inevitable. But it appears worth having gone through them to now be here, with her, like this. Though my head is swelling with a pain that seems raw and idiotic, I feel this intimacy with Carina is my reward.

My reward for the bruises on my chest, the cuts on my neck, the wounds on my shoulders and back. If they have guaranteed this then they all seem worth it. We both now seem to be physically expressing the wounds that our minds have suffered in the past years. It's as if they have all been brought to the surface in a few wild minutes. But now they are worn on the outside of our bodies we can finally tend to them. As I smooth her hair, it feels as if we're finally showing each other honest portraits of ourselves.

I kiss the top of her head, and she looks up at me with a weak smile. I am used to Carina playing the distant seductress, but now she seems completely unmasked. I realise that my life until now has been a hopeless series of wanderings, but now I have a purpose, however long it takes her to accept that. I promise myself that I must not ever shirk this vague and sincere duty.

Her fingers close on my slightly bloodied shirt. "You need to see a doctor," she whispers. "Is your chest still bleeding?"

"I don't like to talk about it," I whisper, with fake-modesty.

She laughs and strokes my chest. "You're a mad little man. Always getting into situations that are out of your depth. In the morning we'll solve everything."

"We'll have to," I say, thinking about the wreckage of the house. Though I know I should check if Barbara's alright, I'm unable to prise myself from our makeshift home.

"I've never been that scared," she says. "It took so long

to be able to walk again after the accident. Months and months of rehab, of excruciating pain just so I could get out of bed in the morning. And I thought that in a moment of madness James might undo all that. With all this anger that is based on nothing. If you hadn't arrived I don't know what would have happened."

"I came in because I heard Georgina and Barbara arguing. I think Georgina may have hit her."

"So it's just luck that brought you downstairs at that moment?"

"Yes."

"When you came through the door, part of me was hugely relieved. But another part of me was more scared that he might hurt you instead."

"I don't think he set out to hurt anyone Carina. He needs help."

She sits up and looks me in the eye, before glancing down at my body. "Of all the people who might have overheard, don't you think it's strange that it was you?"

I look back at her intrigued expression. "It does seem a coincidence. But I don't believe it's anymore than that."

"But... "

She seems hesitant to reveal what is on her mind, and I hope badly it is what I want it to be. I don't know if I can take any more painful blows this evening, in whatever way they manifest themselves.

"But it's not the first time, is it Vincent? It's not the first time you've been the one who's there when I need help."

"Carina, don't tease me with anything, not tonight. Too much has happened."

"I know. I'm sorry. Perhaps I should keep quiet."

She pauses for a second, and then looks back at me again. "Or perhaps I can tell you and promise that it won't hurt?"

"Okay, but I don't think you can promise that."

"I just did."

"Okay then try," I say, focusing on her.

"You've always been in the background, ever since we met. Something in me perhaps wasn't ready to bring you into the foreground. But without asking for anything back you've always been there for me. In a quiet, understated way. I think I've taken it for granted that you'll always be there."

"I'm not sure I follow."

"Just like I took it for granted that life would tend to my every desire. Although in a strange way I think it does. I think that it brought us here, to this situation, with both of us tending to each other's wounds. Don't you think that is a sign, considering what has happened tonight?"

"Yes, I meant what I said in the summer house. But you didn't need to wait for a sign to know that what I said was true."

"Perhaps I did Vincent. Perhaps I'm different to you and can't take hold of my own destiny in the way that you can. Perhaps I needed to be told. But right now, looking at us in this situation, I do think I have been told."

"What are you saying?" The throbbing pain makes it difficult for me to see clearly, and the light from the lamps is painful on my weary eyes. I feel myself pushing through every word to a solution, to the point at which everything will be resolved. I've been drained dry, drained of every drop of emotion and energy, but still feel I must push on. I've reached the summit now, and her company is my prize. I mustn't give up at this point, when we feel so close to a solution – however much my tired body desperately wants me to.

"I'm saying you were right Vincent. What you said in the summer house. We owe it to ourselves to give us a chance. We should just forget about James, and Elise, and even The Intimates if they hold us back."

It surprises me how much it hurts to speak. I am silent for far too long as I try to find the words, and when they do come out I feel sure they are all wrong, that they will only take us back a step and not forward. But nonetheless, I speak. I speak because I know I have to keep trying until my body completely gives up on me.

"Elise is gone," I whisper. "She left me. She told me that she thought I was in love with you."

"And are you?"

She doesn't seem to know how close I am to passing out. She looks up. Looks at me directly, with searching eyes. But this time it's her hand that tends to the side of my face. There's a little smear of dirt just above her mouth, which breaks into a hopeful smile.

"Yes. I am." And then I remember the brief few moments when the pain entirely disappeared, when she leant into my body to kiss me.

As time passes, when the sun tears itself through the shroud of the night, I feel an intense, swinging happiness. It's so unrestrained and unapologetic in its intensity that it almost overwhelms me. Somehow I suspect that I will replay this moment an infinite number of times, always trying to recapture its details in vain. The reassurance of the rising sun, the delicate silence of the garden. Every nerve in my body seems to applaud my actions, which makes me think that I must not suspect her words. People have made infinite promises in the past, which they've broken at the first opportunity, but given all that has happened tonight I feel sure that I should believe her.

Sensing movement from the other end of the garden I realise I can't even move anymore, as my eyes slowly begin to close. I can't even try to defend this time with her, which I know to be so fragile that it could end at any moment. Everything I need is here, and my only ambition now is to keep the two of us hidden from the rest of the world, even while asleep.

It was the sun rising over the copse of trees that made my eyes open again. Carina stayed still and silent in my arms as I gradually stirred awake. For the first time I saw the statues surrounding the pool, each of them covered in an elaborate web of vines and vegetation. Previously the garden had seemed overgrown and dishevelled but, waking up in it, it now seemed perfectly arranged and made to a design that was quite deliberate.

The plants were rich, green and wet with dew. The statues looked over us with a friendly indifference. Somehow our surroundings seemed to have been expecting us. The way Carina shuffled in my arms suggested that this delicate sheen of sunlight had been expected by her too.

Waking up in a strange a place , I should have wanted to leave immediately. But I didn't feel that way at all at the foot of The Fountains. Carina and I seemed to belong amongst its hazy decadence, as much as any of the vines or broken statues. As if greeting me, a thin stream of water careered down the faint, sky blue tiles of the swimming pool and towards my feet. Carina's scent filled my nostrils, invigorating me as I watched the trail of water stall, building into a ripe pool inches from my shoes.

I covered her cheek with my hand and lay back. Although I hadn't quite absorbed Carina's words about fate, the scenery did seem to be whispering something to me. But it was only now, after a night in its company, that I felt able to comprehend what it was trying to say.

Carina and I had long reprimanded ourselves for being damaged, for having passed our peak. But this garden too was damaged, and had long seen better days. And yet it seemed that nothing about it should be altered. One only needed to spend sufficient time in its company to realise that every fault was what made it complete. The garden seemed to be uttering that I never again should desire to be different. That I was exactly what, and where I should be. As if saluting my belated understanding, a smattering of birds rise over the trees, singing out jubilantly. I followed them with my eyes as Carina slowly opened hers.

"How did we get here?" she asked, sitting up and laying her dry lips upon my cheek. I shrugged, and stroked a cut on her arm. "There is something quite beautiful about this garden, isn't there?"

"I doubt if Francoise is aware of that. I don't even think she ever comes down here."

"You're joking, aren't you?" Carina whispered, squinting under the glare of the ever-brightening sun. "Francoise told me yesterday that this is her favourite part of the garden. That her gardener has been tearing his hair out over the state of it, but Francoise insists that it must be kept exactly as it is. That he could not make it more beautiful if he tried. When she told me that I thought she was quite mad. But now I can see that Francoise still has much to teach me."

Something occurs to me, but then I stop myself.

"What?" she asks, addressing a tear in her dress. "You're wondering something, I know you are. You're wondering if Francoise showed you that secret passageway for a reason, aren't you?"

I laugh. "It's too outlandish a thought for serious consideration. Although if what you say is true, then I don't understand why Francoise has not come looking for us down here." I lean over to kiss her but my hand slips and I crumple onto the floor. The pain comes crashing back.

As Carina helps me up I notice that she barely looks dishevelled. The long curls of dark hair and the slightly amused eyes make her look like a fawn that's just appeared from the undergrowth.

"You really need to have your cuts looked at," she says, taking the jacket from her shoulders and placing it around mine. "Should I take you inside, or to a hospital?"

"I'm not sure I need a hospital. But, I'm not entirely sure that going back in there will help my condition."

She adjusts her earrings and rises to her feet. "I agree. In fact, I am reluctant to go back inside there at all."

"Do you remember what we agreed? That we weren't going to be restrained by them anymore?"

"Of course," she answers. "And I stand by that too." Her hands gently touch the marks at my side, and I close my eyes. I imagine her washing me in one of the fountains by the house, splashing water onto my wounds until each is cleared of blood. I picture the dark fan of her hair backlit by the sun as she cranes over me, precisely attending to each wound. The trees rustling in applause as the two of us step out of the fountain and back onto the grass, walking out of the grounds together without once looking back at the house.

It's the blast of white sun overhead, along with the returning pain which makes me regain consciousness. But I don't open my eyes. My body wants to regroup first, to assess how seriously it's been damaged. It takes me a moment to recall where I am. To realise that I'm surrounded by the sky blue tiles of the pool, smooth and glistening around me, like the walls of an oyster shell. Sealing me from the world for a short while until their protection is rendered useless.

The pool had long been drained of any water. All that filled it now were leaves, brittle and gold in the bright morning sun. When I opened my eyes I saw the hollow shell of the pool, its walls stained with algae. I realised that I wasn't alone in its corner, as huddled against my tuxedo was a girl with dark hair, asleep.

Guy Mankowski

Guy was raised on the Isle of Wight before being taught by monks at Ampleforth College, York. After graduating with a Psychology degree from Durham and a Masters from Newcastle University, Guy formed a Dickensian pop band called Alba Nova, releasing one EP. After that he started working as a psychologist at The Royal Hospital in London followed by a psychotherapy clinic in Newcastle.

Guy Mankowski is also a published short story writer – read his work in the short story collections *Eight Rooms* and *Ten Journeys*.

www.guymankowski.blogspot.com

For more info on Legend Press:

www.legendpress.co.uk

www.twitter.com/legend_press

1	2	3	4	5	6	7	8	9	10
11	12	13	14	15	16	17	18	19	20
21	22	23	24	25	26	27	28	29	30
31	32	33	34	35	36	37	38	39	40
41	42	43	44	45	46	47	48	49	50
51	52	53	54	55	56	57	58	59	60
61	62	63	64	65	66	67	68	69	70
71	72	73	74	75	76	77	78	79	80
81	82	83	84	85	86	87	88	89	90
91	92	93	94	95	96	97	98	99	100
101	102	103	104	105	106	107	108	109	110
111	112	113	114	115	116	117	118	119	120
121	122	123	124	125	126	127	128	129	130
131	132	133	134	135	136	137	138	139	140
141	142	143	144	145	146	147	148	149	150
151	152	153	154	155	156	157	158	159	160
161	162	163	164	165	166	167	168	169	170
171	172	173	174	175	176	177	178	179	180
181	182	183	184	185	186	187	188	189	190
191	192	193	194	195	196	197	198	199	200
201	202	203	204	205	206	207	208	209	210
211	212	213	214	215	216	217	218	219	220
221	222	223	224	225	226	227	228	229	230
231	232	233	234	235	236	237	238	239	240
241	242	243	244	245	246	247	248	249	250
251	252	253	254	255	256	257	258	259	260
261	262	263	264	265	266	267	268	269	270
271	272	273	274	275	276	277	278	279	280
281	282	283	284	285	286	287	288	289	290
291	292	293	294	295	296	297	298	299	300
301	302	303	304	305	306	307	308	309	310
311	312	313	314	315	316	317	318	319	320
321	322	323	324	325	326	327	328	329	330
331	332	333	334	335	336	337	338	339	340
341	342	343	344	345	346	347	348	349	350
351	352	353	354	355	356	357	358	359	360
361	362	363	364	365	366	367	368	369	370
371	372	373	374	375	376	377	378	379	380
381	382	383	384	385	386	387	388	389	390
391	392	393	394	395	396	397	398	399	400

Lightning Source UK Ltd.
Milton Keynes UK
UKOW040742020912

198345UK00001B/2/P

9 781907 756467